"It was a long time ago," Chandra murmured as she looked up at Rick.

"But the effects are still with you, and it bothers me. I want so much to touch you without your pulling away from me. See . . ." His hand stroked lightly down her pale hair to her shoulder. ". . . like this. Feel? My touch isn't painful. I would never harm you."

She didn't pull away. She stood very still, barely able to breathe.

His hand brushed across her collarbone. "You're exquisite, Chandra, and I want more than anything to see your glorious hair spread out on my pillow in the morning."

"Stop it," she said, but she whispered.

His fingers paused on the rapid pulse at the base of her throat. "I want you to get used to my touch, Chandra. It tears something apart inside me when you pull away."

"Let me go," she said, although he wasn't holding her.

"I want to kiss you over every inch of your body and have your golden skin melt beneath my lips." He lowered his mouth to press against the place his fingers had touched. "I want to wrap myself in you . . ."

WHAT ARE *LOVESWEPT* ROMANCES?

They are stories of true romance and touching emotion. We believe those two very important ingredients are constants in our highly sensual and very believable stories in the *LOVESWEPT* line. Our goal is to give you, the reader, stories of consistently high quality that may sometimes make you laugh, sometimes make you cry, but are always fresh and creative and contain many delightful surprises within their pages.

ost romance fans read an enormous number of books. Those they ly love, they keep. Others may be traded with friends and soon forgotten. We hope that each *LOVESWEPT* romance will be a treasure—a "keeper." We will always try to publish

LOVE STORIES YOU'LL NEVER FORGET
BY AUTHORS YOU'LL ALWAYS REMEMBER

The Editors

LOVESWEPT® • 199

Fayrene Preston
Allure

BANTAM BOOKS
TORONTO • NEW YORK • LONDON • SYDNEY • AUCKLAND

ALLURE

A Bantam Book / July 1987

LOVESWEPT® and the wave device are registered
trademarks of Bantam Books, Inc. Registered in U.S. Patent
and Trademark Office and elsewhere.

If you would be interested in receiving protective vinyl
covers for your Loveswept books, please write to this address
for information:

Loveswept
Bantam Books
P.O. Box 985
Hicksville, NY 11802

ISBN 0-553-21835-2

Published simultaneously in the United States and Canada

PRINTED IN THE UNITED STATES OF AMERICA

O   0 9 8 7 6 5 4 3 2 1

One

Help! Come as soon as you can.
Someone is trying to drown me!

Chandra Stuart recalled the words of Lillian's cryptic note as she drew closer to Monte Luna, Texas, the town where she had been born and raised, the town she hadn't seen for close to nine years. Aware of how tightly her slender hands were grasping the steering wheel, Chandra deliberately loosened her grip.

As much as she would have liked to kid herself, she knew it wasn't worry over her mother's note that had tied her stomach in knots. Over the years, Chandra had grown accustomed to Lillian's dramatics, and she knew the note wasn't to be taken literally. But then again, her mother had never before asked for her help, and that fact alone had warranted the trip.

Unfortunately there had been no way to call, since Lillian had been conducting a feud with the phone company. Apparently the phone company had won, because when Chandra had tried to call, a recorded message had informed her that the phone had been disconnected.

As a result, she had been driving steadily since early morning, without too many breaks. The wind rushed in through the car's open window, so that her thick, pale blond hair whipped around her head. From a side part her hair billowed with natural body to fall down past her shoulders in soft waves that had never known a perm or a set. Long ago Chandra had accepted that her hair couldn't be forced into anything remotely resembling a tame or fashionable hairstyle. So she let the wind blow, enjoying the air in her hair and against her skin.

Checking the speedometer, she discovered she was driving much too fast, a sure sign she was becoming edgy. Easing off the accelerator, she threw a quick glance over her shoulder at her son, Ty, who was sleeping soundly in the back of the station wagon, surrounded by his beloved Transformers. Long red lashes lay on his lightly freckled cheeks. His red-gold hair glinted with healthy life. Usually he was an eight-year-old whirlwind of motion, but excitement had awakened him early, and the trip halfway across Texas had been boring and tiring for him.

Taking him home to see his grandmother would be good for him, Chandra thought. He was old enough now to make it harder and harder for her to keep coming up with reasons why the only time he got to see his grandmother was when she came to visit them. Why, he had asked more than once, couldn't they go to Grandma's?

Chandra felt herself tensing again. Deliberately she smoothed a finger back and forth across her forehead. After a self-imposed exile from anyplace, a certain amount of apprehension upon return was natural, she told herself. There was no need for her to worry. After all, she had only taken two weeks off from work. What could happen in two weeks?

Ten minutes earlier, Chandra had turned off the interstate, and now she noticed that the outskirts of Monte Luna were coming into view.

It was a strange experience for her to be coming back to the west Texas town where she had grown up. The sights were both familiar, yet not familiar.

Oil, once the king, was now on the decline. On either side of the road, pump heads stood motionless like giant praying mantises. Yet from surface appearances, the economy of the area hadn't seemed to suffer that much. The old drive-in movie had been torn down, and a new development had sprung up, apparently coexisting peacefully with the older, smaller, wood-frame houses that lined the road.

Ahead, on Chandra's left, a billboard proclaimed that Sky Mesa offered luxury estates of five and ten acres. She remembered Sky Mesa very well. It was on the other side of town, and very close to her mother's land. *And once there had been a night . . .*

Chandra deliberately switched her gaze to the gas gauge. Nearly empty. Coming up on her right was a gas station. Quickly making her decision, she slowed and made the turn into the station that had at one time borne the name of Sanchez, but now boasted the name of a major gas chain. A gentle smile lifted the corners of her mouth as she remembered how she and her girlfriend, Pam, had always stopped by Mr. Sanchez's before going to the drive-in movie for the evening—not for gas, but to have the windshield cleaned. And Mr. Sanchez had always cheerfully complied. Now, she noticed, the station was self-service.

Chandra regretted a lot of the new things she was seeing, but she, better than anyone, knew that time brought changes, and she supposed she really couldn't object, when she had undergone so many changes herself.

She pulled the car to a stop and switched off the engine. In the backseat Ty didn't stir, and she decided to let him sleep until they arrived at Lillian's. She opened the car door, stepped out, and gratefully stretched her stiff muscles.

Mid-stretch she froze. For not three feet away, leaning casually against a car, filling it with gas, was Richard O'Neill—the man responsible for her fleeing Monte Luna, the man responsible for her staying away for so long. Her worst fears had been realized, and all in a matter of minutes after driving into town!

She turned away, and, as swiftly as she could, weighed her options. She could see no other way but to go ahead and fill up her car. To leave abruptly might call attention to herself. But if she kept her back to him . . .

Quickly grabbing the pump handle closest to her, she began to try to insert it into her gas tank, but for some reason the nozzle was too big for the opening of her gas tank, and as a result she could only put a small amount of gas into the tank at a time without its spilling over. Silently she cursed. She had never seen a nozzle this big before. Filling her car at this rate would take forever!

"I believe you're using the wrong pump," a pleasant voice said.

She started, whipped her head around, and encountered the hazel eyes of Richard O'Neill. At the moment, bits of humor were highlighting their gold-green color she remembered so well. The sight of him was almost too much for her. She couldn't seem to assimilate the shock of his presence. It was as if he had been manifested out of her worries and fears, she thought, then wondered if that was really possible.

"I'd be glad to help."

"What?"

"Your car takes unleaded," he explained patiently. "You're trying to fill it with leaded."

She had no idea what he was saying to her. A roaring had come up in her ears, and her mind and body were busy dealing with the shock of seeing him after all these years.

Richard O'Neill, the town's golden boy. He had lettered in every sport the high school offered, and had gone on to become an All-American football player at the University of Texas. The richest kid in town, he had also been the wildest. His father's wealth had given him extraordinary privilege, and he had taken full advantage of it. Guys had followed where he led; girls had come at the crook of his finger. She had been one of those girls.

When Chandra made no move to exchange the pump handle for the proper one, Richard reached for it. At the brush of his hand against hers, she jerked violently, causing gas to spray across his tan-colored slacks and strong fumes to fill the air.

"Oh, I'm sorry!"

Carefully, as if it were a lethal weapon, Rick took the gas nozzle from her. "I'll be all right as long as you don't decide to light a match." His mouth crooked engagingly. "You don't smoke, do you?" he asked in mock concern.

She shook her head, dazed by the fact that his easy grin had moved something in her that hadn't been moved in an awfully long time.

He hung up the pump handle she had been trying to use and reached for the handle of the unleaded gas. "Let me help you."

Slowly she came out of her daze. "There's really no need to do that. I can manage now."

His body grazed hers as he inserted the proper-sized nozzle into her car's gas tank and set the handle on automatic. She took a few steps to the side to draw his gaze away from the car. The ploy worked.

Rick's eyes sparkled with interest as they expertly took in everything about her. It was obvious to him that she had dressed for comfort. Her faded jeans fit her long legs and gently rounded hips closely and with a well-worn familiarity. The pink cotton-knit tank top lovingly hugged high, firm breasts, which clearly weren't confined by a bra. And her hair . . . her hair . . .

"Don't you believe in relying on the kindness of strangers?" he asked.

Two things registered with her at once. He was flirting with her. And more importantly, *he didn't remember her!* She might have laughed if for some strange reason she hadn't felt like crying. Instead of doing either, she answered him. "I've always found it best to rely only on myself. It's so much safer that way."

He smiled slowly. "I'm sure that's very wise—in most cases. But in this case you can depend on me. I'm not at all dangerous."

I don't believe you, she thought, returning his smile with one that was absolutely devoid of any sincerity, *because I have every reason to know that you are extremely dangerous.* She pushed her hands into the pockets of her jeans, willed her gas tank to fill quickly, and tried to busy her mind with something other than the man before her. It didn't work.

Richard O'Neill hadn't grown any taller, but his athlete's body had filled out, become harder, more powerful. He wore his copper-hued brown hair longer now. His chest had widened, the muscles of his thighs thickened. The hand that held the gas pump was big and strong . . . and bore no wedding ring.

She didn't need the rapid beating of her heart to tell her that his charisma had increased. When he had been a young man, sexuality had lay just under his skin, and he had accepted and used it with the cocky assurance of youth. Now that sexuality ran marrow-deep, and was all the more potent because he no longer seemed to be aware of it. But she was aware of it.

He had become a man, a devastating man.

He had also become an observant man.

His glance took in the luggage rack on the roof of the station wagon, where three suitcases and a bicycle were strapped down, then went to the back window, through which he could see her sleeping son. "Looks like the two of you have traveled a long way today. Do you have much farther to go?"

"No. Not far at all." She needed to leave, and as soon as possible.

He tilted his head to one side in a mannerism she had once thought so charming. "I don't guess I could be lucky enough to have you stopping in town."

"As a matter of fact, we are." With a natural gesture she tossed her head just as a breeze came up that flung out strands of her hair to the light. "That's enough gas. Thanks for the help."

His eyes narrowed as his gaze went to her hair, then back to her face. "You know, there's something familiar about you. . . ."

"Really?" Her polite smile should have told him that she was uninterested in any come-on lines he might try on her. She reached for the handle of the gas pump, intending to make a gracious yet quick escape. But her hand accidentally brushed his, and she jerked away, deeply disturbed. There had been heat in that touch, and there shouldn't have been.

"Wait a minute! Don't I know you?"

"I . . ." She shook her head, unsure what to say.

He stared at her hair, then snapped his fingers. "Of course! You're Chandra Johnson!" A delighted grin creased his face. "I'm Richard O'Neill."

There had to be humor somewhere in this situation, she thought, but unfortunately she couldn't see it. Never in her worst nightmares had she imagined herself in a position where the man who had shattered her heart would be introducing himself to her.

He hung up the pump and held out his hand. Automatically she found herself extending her own. When he gripped hers, though, she immediately pulled back. Heat—too much to absorb with any degree of comfort.

He didn't seem to notice. "It was your hair that I finally recognized. It's such an unusual color. I'm surprised I didn't guess sooner." He shook his head as if amazed. "Good grief, it's been a long time! How long has it been?"

Eight years, seven months. "I have no idea."

"I'm sorry I didn't recognize you."

Her chin lifted defensively, wishing he would wipe that wonderful smile off his face. "There's no reason why you should have. After all, we hardly knew each other, and you were several years ahead of me in school."

"I guess that's true. It just seems . . ."

"By the way, I'm Chandra Stuart now."

"You're married?" The interest in his eyes didn't diminish, but his tone lost its animation.

"I was at one time."

"Divorced?"

Reluctantly she nodded, her nerves tightening as the strain of the meeting began to tell on her.

"I'm sorry. Where are you living now?"

Unthinkingly she blurted out, "You can't possibly be interested!"

"Why wouldn't I be interested?"

He appeared to be genuinely bewildered, but she knew better. Rick O'Neill was not to be trusted.

"I'm living in Shreveport," she finally answered.

"Doing what?"

"I'm a buyer for a department store there."

"Really?" His eyebrows raised consideringly.

In the back of the station wagon, Ty rolled over. He nodded toward the sleeping child. "And he's your son?"

Now he was on dangerous ground. "That's right. Look, thanks again for the help, but I've really got to be going."

He nodded. "I guess you're anxious to get out to your mother's." Tilting his head to regard her, he asked, "That is why you're here, isn't it? To visit her?"

"She is the only reason I would ever come back for a visit," Chandra said with more force than she had intended or than was necessary.

"That's good. I'm sure we'll be seeing each other."

"I doubt it, but it was nice seeing you again." With Rick's curious gaze following her, she hurried to the cashier's window and paid, then walked back to the car, climbed in, and drove away.

Watching her go, his own half-filled car forgotten for the moment, Rick decided that there was no doubt he would see Chandra Stuart again. From the first moment he had turned around and seen her, working so hard to fill her car with the wrong gas, he had wanted to know who she was. And then it turned out he had known her, or, he corrected himself, at least known *of* her.

Even though Chandra had been three grades behind him, he had been aware of her. He remembered her hair, blowing about her head in such a wild and natural way. He also remembered how every time he happened to cast his gaze her way, she always seemed to be watching him with those wide blue eyes of hers. He had been vaguely intrigued, but she had been too young.

Then she had been a pretty, romantic-looking girl. Now she was a ravishing beauty. Then and now she was totally different from her mother.

He, like everyone in town, knew her mother. Lillian Johnson was an artist whose paintings of their area had attained a cult following over the years. Lillian Johnson was also a difficult, stubborn, eccentric, reclusive woman, who was currently giving him and the entire town problems. He hoped Chandra's visit would help the situation.

A new thought struck him, causing him to frown. Chandra had been in a hurry to leave, unusually so. He had supposed she was just anxious to get to Lillian's. Yet there had been a wariness in her eyes. No woman had ever looked at him in such a way.

He shrugged away the feeling of disquiet. He would see her again. He would make sure he did.

Chandra pulled the station wagon into the yard and parked beside Lillian's old Chrysler sedan. Turning the engine off, she sat for a moment. A lump that wouldn't be dislodged came up in her throat as she took in the place where she had been born and raised.

Most people would say it was nothing special, she supposed. The house was a typical two-story wooden farm house with a chimney at each end and a long porch on the front. A studio had been added onto the back of it when she had been around Ty's age, but it couldn't be seen from the front.

Close to a hundred acres surrounded the house, most of them allowed to go back to scrub long ago. But the immediate yard was a nicely kept lawn, and a flower bed that ran the length of the front porch held shrubs and flowers.

In fact, Chandra was amazed. Everything was in such terrific condition, it was too good to be

Lillian's work. For even as a young girl, it had fallen to Chandra to see that the needed repairs were taken care of. Lillian simply didn't care what things looked like. Only her art, her daughter, and her grandson were important enough to warrant her attention.

Chandra reched over her seat to shake Ty gently. "Wake up, honey. We're here."

The slamming of a screen door brought her attention back to the house. Dressed in her usual mannishly cut pants and shirt, Lillian stood on the front porch, her hands resting on her slim hips. She was a tall woman, with broad shoulders and long gray hair that each day she twisted without fanfare into a bun. Although there was nothing at all feminine about her, Lillian possessed a definite regalness that kept most people at arm's length. But there had never been a doubt in Chandra's mind that her mother loved her and that, no matter what mistakes she might make in her life, Lillian was one person she could count on never to change, never to stop loving her.

Chandra smiled, stepped out of the car, and waved. "Hi, Lillian!" She had forgotten just when it was she had stopped calling Lillian "Mom." She was simply Lillian, and Chandra was certain that God had broken the mold when he had made her.

"Where's that grandson of mine?" Lillian called.

"Grandma!" Ty bounded out of the car and raced across the yard and up the steps to his grandmother's waiting arms.

"How's my Ty?" Lillian asked, sweeping him up into an exuberant hug that nearly smothered him.

"Great! I'm out of school for the summer! Is this your house?"

"It sure is. What do you think of it?"

"It's great! Do you have any horses I can ride?"

"No, but just say the word, and I'll buy one for you."

"Wow!"

"Lillian!" Chandra had just reached the porch, and had heard her mother's last statement.

"Go on in and look around, Ty, while I say hello to your mother." Lillian's lively eyes turned on her daughter, and she pulled her into her arms for a hug equal to the one she had given Ty. "And how's my Chandra?"

"I'm fine." She drew back, tried to give her mother a stern look, and failed. "And evidently you are too."

Lillian had no trouble giving Chandra a stern once-over. "You're too thin, of course, but you always were scrawny. Such frail bones. Nothing I could do about it, though. The only thing I can figure out is that you must be a throwback on your father's side."

"Never mind that. Just tell me what all this nonsense is about someone trying to drown you."

"It's not nonsense!" Lillian's entire demeanor changed and her voice rose, quivering with a fine rage. "Someone *is* trying to drown me, and I'll tell you all about it as soon as I get you and Ty settled."

Chandra had a multitude of questions, but they waited, because her mother opened the screen door and pushed her inside the house, where a sense of coming home immediately overwhelmed

ALLURE • 15

her. The high-ceilinged rooms seemed to hold the
same old clutter. Patterned curtains, familiar but
faded, fluttered at the long windows. Family pictures lined the pine mantle. In one corner of the
room her dad's baby grand sat, unused since her
dad had died of pneumonia when she had been
seven years old.

So much the same, she thought. Yet even here
in the home she loved so much she found changes.
Unless she was very much mistaken, the walls
had been replastered and painted cream. The
wooden floors had been stripped and refinished,
so that they shone with a luster she had never
seen. The furniture did seem to be in the same
place, although a few pieces had been reuphol-
stered.

But there was no doubt about it, she was home.
If nothing else, the smells would have told her
so—something delicious simmering on the stove,
the faint scent of paints from Lillian's attached
studio, the stronger aroma of coffee brewing.

Tuning out Ty's and Lillian's happy chatter,
Chandra made her way up to the room she had
slept in for the first seventeen years of her life.
Here she found no changes. The same brightly
patterned quilt covered the bed. The same deli-
cately figured lace curtains hung at the two wide
windows that met in one corner, although she
could tell the curtains had been recently washed
and ironed.

Beneath the windows was a padded window
seat, where, as a young girl, she had sat for hours,
dreaming of things that, as it turned out, were

never to be. Slowly, inexorably drawn, she walked to her dresser. She opened a bottom drawer and found, buried beneath neatly folded sweaters left behind so long ago, a stack of newspaper clippings.

Now yellowed and frayed, each of the newspaper clippings told a story about the same subject—Richard O'Neill. Some were just pictures, including the one taken of him still in his football uniform after a big game. Others were articles, such as the one written when he made All-American. There was even an announcement that had told the town he would be going off to college. She slammed the drawer shut and sank onto the edge of the bed.

She had first noticed Rick when she was fourteen and he was seventeen and a senior in high school. Love had come quick and hard. Or at least at that age it had seemed like love to her. Now she saw it for what it had been—a huge crush.

But her teenaged feelings had run strong. To her, he had been the epitome of everything a boy should be: good-looking, smart, popular, sexy. She had known nothing about sex—not then, at any rate.

She seized every opportunity to be where he was, so that she could watch him. She memorized his smile and his gestures. She studied the way he talked to a girl and how the girl responded. Then she would come home and practice in front of the mirror until she was sure that if he ever talked to her, she would know just what to do.

Rick graduated and went off to the University of Texas, and Chandra started living from holiday to holiday and summer to summer, because those were the times when Rick was home. And no one ever knew—not her mother, who, as long as Chandra was healthy and happy, gave most of her attention to her art, and not Chandra's friends, who giggled and talked of clothes, makeup, and boys their own age.

But all of that changed the night Chandra graduated. The country club had been decorated with tiny lights and silver and blue streamers. Lillian had bought Chandra a beautiful aqua dress that brought out the turquoise tone in her blue eyes. The dress was strapless and made out of a frothy organdy. She remembered laughing and dancing with first one boy and then another.

And then Rick and his friends had walked in, crashing the party. No one had minded, of course. The high-school kids felt that having college men at their party elevated it. And the management of the country club didn't mind, because Rick's father was on the board of directors and a charter member.

Chandra had retreated to a corner to watch as Rick grabbed a girl and took her out on the dance floor. Looking back on that night, she realized that he had already had quite a bit to drink by the time he arrived, and in the next hour he drank even more from several bottles he and his friends had brought in with them. But at the time she had never been around anyone who drank, so she didn't recognize the signs.

Besotted, she didn't take her eyes off him, or at least she didn't think she did, but suddenly she looked up and he was standing in front of her.

"You look like a Raphaelite angel," he mumbled, "with all that wild, glorious hair." He tilted his head consideringly. "Are you as wild and glorious, I wonder?"

All the hours of practicing before the mirror failed her. Her heart was pounding too hard for her to answer. He laughed. "Dance with me?"

She nodded.

Ever afterward, she had never been able to recall how long they had danced. Maybe it hadn't been long at all. But she did remember when he had kissed her neck. Tingles of heat had shot all over her body.

"Lord, but you smell good!" he'd murmured. "Is that perfume or is that you?" When she hadn't answered, he pulled away and gazed down into her eyes. "Will you come with me?"

Staring spellbound up into his beautiful hazel eyes, which seemed pure gold at the moment, she hadn't been able to do anything else but nod.

They had driven out to Sky Mesa, much too fast, but the speed had only added to the excitement that was racing through her veins. The top was down on his convertible and the wind had whipped around them. In the distance, heat lightning scored the horizon, adding a dimension of electricity to the sensational night. Apprehension had churned in the pit of her stomach, but the exhilaration of actually being with Rick won out.

When he pulled to a stop on the mesa, it seemed

to her that they were at the edge of the world. Around them it was a night brilliant and full-blown, a night when dreams surely would come true.

He had spread a blanket over the grass, and she had known a moment's panic, but then he reached for her and she knew no more fear. There, beneath a sky filled with lightning and stars, Rick O'Neill had taken her virginity.

Two

"Mom! Mom!"

Ty's excited voice snapped Chandra out of her reverie. "I'm in here, honey."

Ty burst through the door, full of excitement and energy. "Where have you been? Grandma has been showing me around her studio, and it's so great. I wanted you to see it."

"I'm sorry, honey. I guess I was a little tired after the trip."

"You were resting?"

It was difficult to lie to Ty, especially when he looked at her with those clear blue eyes that were so much like her own. He was such a sweet child, she thought, her heart swelling with love. He considered it his job to look after her. She was his only parent, since he barely remembered Don.

"Do you like my room?" she asked, changing the subject.

"I suppose," he said consideringly, glancing around. "It doesn't look like your room at home."

"That's because I'm a different person than when I lived here."

"How are you different?"

That was her son, Chandra thought wryly. Always asking the tough questions. "Well, for one thing, I'm all grown up now. Has Grandma showed you the room you'll be sleeping in?"

He nodded. "It's right down the hall."

"Good. What's Grandma doing?"

"Fixin' supper."

"Well, then, I think I'll go down and help. Why don't you unpack?"

Ty's face fell. "I wanted to go outside and look around. Grandma said there's some stables and a barn."

"There are, but I don't think they've been used in years. You shouldn't go out there by yourself."

"Aw, Mom, it'll be okay."

"You can't go until I know what kind of shape things are in out there, and that's that," Chandra said firmly. "Now, let's go see what Grandma's cooking."

Later that night, with Ty in his pajamas and settled in front of the television set in the living room, Chandra waited for her mother to tell her who was trying to drown her.

Lillian stood in the middle of the kitchen, puffing furiously on a cigarette. Another cigarette burned in an ashtray across the room. Lillian's habit of lighting cigarettes and then forgetting them had always driven Chandra crazy, but she had long ago accepted that there was nothing she could do about it, and cigarette burns on the carpets, furniture, and counters bore witness to the fact.

"It's that Richard O'Neill!" Lillian suddenly said, jolting Chandra. The hot coffee she was drinking sloshed over the rim of the cup onto her hand. "He's the one who's behind this lake project that will flood my land, if it's put in."

"A lake project?" Chandra asked a bit helplessly, sucking the coffee off the reddened skin of her hand.

"That's right. And of course everyone is following him like lambs to the slaughter, believing every word he says, as if he's some modern-day prophet."

"What exactly is it that he's saying?"

"Stuff and nonsense about the lake's being good for the town."

Chandra frowned. "I don't understand. The Rick O'Neill I knew ten years ago couldn't have cared less about this town. He was too interested in having a good time. Why would he want a lake to go in here?"

"Money!" Lillian lit another cigarette. "As if he doesn't have enough already!"

"He certainly should have," Chandra said slowly, trying to make sense of what her mother was saying. "He would have inherited everything when his father died, and his father had millions."

"Of course"—Lillian paused to blow out a thin stream of smoke—"I must say, the boy has done a lot for the town."

Chandra was confused. "He has?"

Although Lillian's point of view had just taken a right turn, it didn't take her long to get it back on track. "But the town has had enough done for it. Now he's trying to throw me off my land, and *that* I won't stand for. This lake will be fine for him; he won't lose one acre of land! Well, if he wants a fight, I'll give him one, and I want you to help me."

"Look, Lillian, I'll help all I can. I've taken two weeks off from the store, but to tell you the truth, I'd rather not have anything to do with Rick."

"Why?"

She was surrounded by people who asked tough questions, she thought, suddenly realizing how very tired she was. But she answered as truthfully as she could, given the situation. "I never really knew him."

"What's to know? He's a spoiled rich kid."

"He's not a kid any longer," Chandra pointed out. "He's thirty-one now."

"He is?" Lillian asked, glancing around for her pack of cigarettes. "Well, the point is, you don't have to like him or even have anything to do with him. Go see your friend Pam tomorrow. I'll bet she can give you the lowdown. Her husband, Robert, is in partnership with Richard."

"Pam? I haven't heard from her in a while."

"Then you probably don't know. They're living out on Sky Mesa now."

Sky Mesa was just a few miles away from Lillian's, and looked eastward over the town of Monte Luna. Taking the road that climbed gently upward toward the new development, Chandra couldn't help but marvel at the beautiful estates that had been built, all carefully placed and landscaped so as to be in total harmony with the land that lay around them.

One home caught her attention more than the others, so much so that she stopped to admire it. It was perched on the edge of the mesa, so that the back of the house would have a magnificent view of the town below it and the front of the house looked out over the plains that rolled westward and upward, eventually reaching to the Permian basin.

The architectural design of the two-story house was stunningly strong, yet it looked perfectly at home where it stood, as if it had just swept in off the prairie with the west Texas wind.

Even before she looked up to see the name, O'Neill, printed on the arch above the two stone gates, she had known it was Rick's house.

Then a sudden realization hit her. His estate encompassed the place where the two of them would have lain that night so long ago, that night that had altered the course of her life.

*　　*　　*

The night wind had been gentle; Rick had been rough. There had been pain, but, in her youth, she had welcomed it, because Rick was the boy she loved and now he would love her too.

And there had also been pleasure, fleeting and brief, but enough so that she had received a glimpse of what it would be like the next time they made love. When he had rolled off her and fallen asleep, she had snuggled against him and waited for the moment when he would awake and again take her in his arms.

The realization that he wasn't going to wake up came to her gradually. Her watch told her that it was late, and she knew Lillian would be worried, so she rearranged her beautiful organdy dress and, on the most important night of her life, walked home alone.

Chandra looked up one more time at the name O'Neill on the arch above the two stone gates, then pressed her foot to the accelerator to drive on.

"I can't tell you how happy I am that you've come back at last," Pam said, beaming at Chandra with the smile that had had almost every member of the football team following her around like a puppy when she had been in high school.

"I'll only be here for two weeks," Chandra said, "but you're right, this visit is long overdue."

"You know I've always wondered why you didn't

come back home to live after your divorce," Pam said contemplatively. "I know Lillian wanted you to."

Chandra gave a short laugh. "She used every device she could dream up to get me to return here, but by that time Shreveport was home, I guess, and I had gotten a really good job at the store. I don't know." Chandra shrugged, uncomfortable about having to come up with a half-truth in answer. "At any rate, you're looking awfully good."

That brought a huge laugh from Pam. "Are you kidding?" She patted her nicely rounded stomach. "With Junior kicking around in here?"

"Junior? Do you know the baby's going to be a boy?"

"Not really. Just a feeling. What with our terrible Tiffany, over there"—she nodded toward a tiny, curly-haired little girl playing in a sandbox to the side of the shaded patio—"I figure this one is going to be Junior."

"And what does Robert think?"

"He thinks I'm marvelous."

Chandra laughed. "I should hope so!" Her gaze swept around the patio where they were sitting. When Chandra arrived, Pam had proudly given her a tour of her home, a home she had clearly decorated with love and comfort in mind. Blooming plants, colorful furniture, and soft baby toys abounded. "It's lovely here, really lovely," she said. "You and your family must be very happy living here."

"We are. The mesa is a wonderful place for kids,

lots of sunshine and clean air. When the kids are older, we'll put in a swimming pool. I don't know if you remember, but all of this land up here on the mesa was Rick O'Neill's. When he decided he wanted to build here, he asked Robert to come in with him to provide his architectural expertise. It's been a partnership that's profited everyone. By the way, you should see Rick's house. It's a real showplace."

"I saw the outside of it as I was driving here. And speaking of Richard O'Neill"—she hesitated, then decided on the direct approach—"Lillian was telling me last night about a lake project he's behind."

"I bet she was," Pam said, reaching for her glass of lemonade. She threw Chandra a speculative look before taking a sip. "What did she tell you?"

"That he was trying to drown her."

Pam went off into a peal of laughter that soon had her clutching her stomach.

"Don't do that," Chandra ordered, both amused and alarmed, "or I'll be driving you to the hospital!"

"I'm sorry." Pam gasped. "But that sounds so much like Lillian." She took several sips of lemonade, then set the glass down. "Okay, look, here's the story. The lake is going to be built. It's definite. Our town has been working with the state Water Development Board and environmental groups for months now. The bond issue has already been passed to raise the money. All the other owners concerned have already sold their land and will be moving soon."

Chandra couldn't believe what she was hearing. "You mean it's gone that far?"

"That's right. The time for Lillian to protest was back a year or so ago, when the discussions were underway and the decisions were being made. It's too late now, Chandra. Your mother will move one way or the other."

"What do you mean?"

"The right of eminent domain authorizes the taking of private property for public use, with, of course, just compensation being given to the owner. The lake has been judged good for all concerned, and so, one eccentric lady will be removed, by force if necessary."

Chandra groaned, closed her eyes, and leaned her head against the back of the rattan chair.

"And as for its being Rick's fault," she heard Pam continue, "it's true that he's more or less been the force pushing the lake through the necessary stages. But, Chandra, he's done it for the town, and he's been totally honest every step of the way. Many times he's tried to talk to Lillian, but she just couldn't be bothered to listen. You know how she is."

Chandra sighed. Yes, she knew. Opening her eyes, she looked at Pam. "Is it true that this lake is going to benefit him?"

"It's going to benefit us all." Pam leaned forward with an earnest expression on her face. "Chandra, in these years since his father's death, Rick has really worked for this town. It's been thanks to him, mainly, that the drop in oil prices hasn't hurt our economy that much. Practically single-handedly he's lured industries to our town that once wouldn't have thought of building here. But businessmen want towns to offer them more than land before they locate. Among other things, they want a good educational system, but primarily they want a town that's going to grow with them. The lake will be a blessing in a lot of ways. With a continuing influx of people, our water problem would become severe. The lake will solve that, besides providing a great recreational park. There's a possibility of tourism, with fishermen and boaters we've never had before."

Chandra's head was spinning. Why couldn't things ever be simple? she wondered. Why couldn't she have had a quiet two weeks at home, without complications?

"I'm sorry, but you wanted the facts."

Chandra shook her head ruefully. "I had no idea."

"Oh, dear." Pam's attention had been diverted by her increasingly fretful daughter. "I think Tiffany has had enough. Let me take her in and put her down for her morning nap. Just sit here, and I'll be back in a minute." She walked to the sandbox and scooped up her sand-covered daughter.

"Don't feel you need to hurry," Chandra urged. She needed the time to assimilate what she had learned.

"Hello, ladies."

Chandra didn't have to turn toward the masculine voice to know who had spoken, but for some disturbing reason she turned anyway.

Pam's face lit up at the sight of Rick just walking out the door of the house and onto the patio. "Hi! How was your golf game with my husband?"

Rick's eyes sought out Chandra. "Great! He let me win."

"Oh, sure, he did. Robert *lives* for those rare times when he beats you. At any rate, you can keep Chandra company while I take Tiffany in." Suddenly she looked from one to the other. "Oh, I'm sorry, I'm just assuming that you two have met."

Rick walked to where Chandra was sitting and smiled down at her, though he answered Pam. "We have, yesterday when Chandra was driving into town."

"Super. Did Robert come in with you?"

Rick nodded, but his gaze never left Chandra.

"Then I'll see you two in a few minutes. Rick, help yourself to some lemonade. There are extra glasses on the tray, there."

"Thanks." He waited until he heard the glass door slide close, then took the chair beside Chandra. "How are you? I was hoping to see you again."

It was strange, she thought, how softly he spoke to her—strange and unnerving. "I'm fine."

"I tried to call you, but evidently there's a problem with Lillian's phone."

She nodded. "I'm having the phone reconnected this afternoon, which reminds me—I was just about to leave."

She started to rise, but he laid his hand on her arm. "Please, stay, at least for a little while." It wasn't so much the arm she pulled away that made Rick notice, but that she had done it so abruptly, almost violently. But with only a moment's pause he continued. "If I hadn't seen you here, I would have driven out to your mother's this afternoon."

"Why?"

She was looking at him in that wary way of hers, he mused, as if she thought he might pounce on her and eat her. And maybe she wasn't far off the mark, because every time he looked at her, hunger knotted in his stomach, and he couldn't seem to keep his gaze from roving over her. Her flaxen hair was magnificent, as usual, rippling in soft waves around her face and down past her shoulders. Her skin was golden. She wore a simple cotton-knit shift that left her arms and enticingly shaped legs bare, and its clear blue color picked up and intensified the blue of her eyes. On her feet, leather sandals revealed toenails painted a bright coral. The color matched the polish on her fingernails, he saw as he brought his gaze back up her body to her eyes once again.

The lady could turn his world upside down with absolutely no effort, he decided, and found that he didn't care at all.

"Have dinner with me tonight."

"I beg your pardon?"

He could tell from the sound in her voice that his invitation had surprised her, and was amused. Didn't she realize how attracted he was to her? "I'd like to get to know you better."

"Why?"

"Isn't that obvious?"

She studied him for a moment, as if she were

trying to figure something out. Patiently he waited for her decision. When it came, he didn't like it at all.

"I can't have dinner with you tonight," she said, and stood up.

He stood up, too, so fast that he almost knocked her down. He grabbed her, and for a few heartbeats they were very close, so close that her perfume engulfed him in a cloud that seemed to be made up of white flowers, a heavy portion of sensuality, a dash of the moon's mystique, and a splattering of a star-filled heaven. How could that be? he wondered. It was broad daylight. He inhaled deeply, feeling the perfume and the effects of her nearness enter his brain with an explosion.

Then she twisted out of his arms.

Bemused and bewildered, he asked, "What *is* that scent you're wearing?"

"What?" Why didn't he ever say what she expected him to say? Chandra wondered, breathing unevenly, trying to tell herself that the feel of his hard body pressed against hers hadn't affected her.

"Your perfume," he said in a low, growly voice that sounded to her as if it were dark and supple and capable of pulling her into a place she didn't want to be. "It's wonderful and quite unique. I don't think I've ever smelled it before, yet it's vaguely familiar to me."

Emotionally off-balance, she shook her head vehemently. "That's impossible! You couldn't ever have smelled it before. It's a special perfume that my aunt Loraine had made up for me on my sixteenth birthday."

"What's the name of it?"

She hesitated, embarrassed to tell him. "Aunt Loraine named it 'Chandra's Allure.' "

"Perfect," he murmured. "Just perfect." He reached to brush the back of his hand down her cheek.

As if he had struck her, she jerked away. Frowning, he shoved his hands in his pants pockets. "What's wrong, Chandra? You can't seem to stand my touching you. Do you think I might hurt you?"

No, she thought angrily, *you won't. Never again.*

He tilted his head, considering. "Is it because of Lillian and her attitude toward the lake project?"

She wished that he wouldn't use that soft, caressing tone with her, as if he thought that to speak any louder might bruise her. "Can't you just take no for an answer?"

"I can. I have in the past. But regarding you . . . I don't think so."

Something hard inside her was in danger of melting. She could sense it and was frightened. "Rick, dinner or any other thing between us is out of the question. I'm leaving now."

She picked up her purse and got two whole steps away from him before he spoke again.

"I'd like a chance to explain about the lake to you. I've tried to talk to Lillian, but the last time I was out there she chased me away with a shotgun."

She whirled around to face him, horrified. "A shotgun!"

He grinned. "Your mother can be very persuasive when she sets her mind to it."

"I don't know what to say. I'm sorry."

His grin vanished. "Chandra, it looks like it's going to be up to you to convince Lillian that she must move. The whole town feels really bad about her having to relocate, and no one knows quite what to do. But we all know that something is going to have to happen soon. One woman, even a woman as formidable as Lillian Johnson, can't stand in the way of progress."

Chandra gnawed on her bottom lip, her heart going out to her mother. She understood Lillian completely. She also admired her. But this was one fight she was quite certain Lillian was going to lose.

"Please have dinner with me," Rick added on a soft breath.

But she heard him, and so did Pam, just coming out the door, with her husband, Robert, right behind her.

"What a good idea!" Pam exclaimed. "Chandra has been gone so long, she's lost touch and doesn't know that many people anymore. Robert and I were thinking of throwing a party for her."

"Oh, no, that would be too much trouble!" Chandra protested.

"Nonsense," Robert said, placing his arm around his wife's shoulder. "We'd love it, and we insist. In the meantime, you couldn't be in better hands than Rick's."

Rick walked to her side, but was careful not to

touch her. "Then it's settled. I'll pick you up around seven."

She had been neatly painted into a corner, and for the life of her she could see no way out. "I think it would be better if I met you somewhere."

A wonderfully deep laugh erupted from Rick's chest. "Maybe you're right, considering Lillian's disposition these days. Come to my house." He dug in his pocket for a pen and paper. "I'll give you the address."

"That's okay. I know where it is." She didn't care if he heard the distinct lack of enthusiasm in her voice, but she hoped that Pam and Robert hadn't caught it. She turned to them with a warm smile. "I'll see you two soon."

"We'll be in touch about the party," Pam said. "We'll invite Lillian. It will do her good to get out. And next time you come, I want you to bring Ty. I'm dying to see him. Come on, I'll walk you to your car."

Three

"You're having dinner with Richard O'Neill!"

Warningly Chandra held up a finger. "You just climb right down off your high horse, Lillian, and tell me why you chased him off with a shotgun."

Lillian reached for her pack of cigarettes. "I was busy and didn't want to talk to him."

"You mean you didn't want to hear what he had to say to you."

Lillian shrugged, exhaling a stream of smoke from a newly lit cigarette. "Same thing."

Chandra walked around the room and put out two other cigarettes in two different ashtrays. "How could you let things get so far without at least finding out what was going on?"

"I was busy. Besides, I have no intention of moving, so it doesn't make any difference what his or this town's plans are."

"Lillian . . ." Compassion stopped the strong words that Chandra had been about to say. She walked to her mother and laid her hand on her arm. "You're going to have to move, you know. You have no choice. It's the law."

"Laws can be changed. People can be bought. If you'd come home a long time ago, the way I wanted you to, you could have taken care of this."

Chandra sighed. In her own way, Lillian was right. Chandra had long ago accepted that her mother lived in a world in which, most of the time, she could see only her painting. She *did* need someone to take care of her. Which brought to mind a question she had been meaning to ask. "Who's been taking care of this place?"

"Oh"—Lillian waved a hand dismissively—"just Nolan."

"And who's 'just Nolan'?"

Lillian shrugged. "A man who showed up around here a few years ago and asked if he could do odd jobs. I thought, why not? Since you'd gone, the place had gotten pretty run down."

Chandra grinned at her mother's attempt to make her feel guilty. "It must have looked pretty bad around here for you to notice."

Lillian glared at her. "At any rate, Nolan comes over every day or two. You'll probably see him around. He doesn't bother me, and I let him do whatever he thinks needs doing."

"Sounds like a pretty nice arrangement all the way around, but what do you know about him?"

"What's to know? He lives around here somewhere, does good work, and hardly charges anything at all."

"Really?" Chandra made a mental note to find out about Nolan. "Then why haven't you asked Nolan to take care of this 'bothersome lake project' for you?"

Lillian's hand, holding yet another cigarette, paused halfway to her lips, and a frown creased her forehead. "I tried, but for some reason Nolan seems to want me to move."

Ty popped into the room. "Mom, I've already had supper. Can I have a glass of milk?"

"Of course you can, Ty," Lillian said, thoughts of Nolan quickly relegated to the unimportant. "And maybe some cookies?" She arched a questioning eyebrow at Chandra, appearing to ask her permission, but in reality already reaching for the cookie jar.

"Sure," Chandra said with amused resignation, hooking her son around the neck and pulling him to her for a quick hug.

Lillian set a plate of cookies and a glass of milk on the table for Ty. Chandra discreetly reduced the number of cookies by half. Ty settled happily in front of the still-heaped plate.

"At any rate," Lillian said, patting him on the head in approval, "getting back to your dinner date with Richard—"

"I told you, I was forced into it. Besides, in view of your position here, I need to find out all I can about the lake."

"Are you going out tonight, Mom?" Ty asked.

"Don't talk with your mouth full, honey, and yes, I am."

"With a perfectly despicable man," Lillian told him.

Ty looked up with interest. "What's des-pic-a-ble mean?"

"It means he's not very nice," Lillian said.

Chandra frowned at her mother. "It means that he is not letting your grandmother have her way in something."

"Chandra, for the life of me I don't know how you can take sides against your own mother like this."

"I'm not. I just feel that you could have handled this matter in a better way, that's all. And that now you're going to have to resign yourself to moving."

"I will not!"

"You're going to have to move, Grandma?"

"Richard O'Neill wants me to. The man is *pond scum*." Lillian turned toward Chandra. "Did he tell you where he was living now?"

"Yes, on Sky Mesa. I saw the house today. It's spectacular."

"I've heard about it. One man doesn't need such a big place, but I suppose it's just that O'Neill ego. I heard he even has gates at the beginning of his drive with his name on an arch above them." She poured Ty some more milk. "Well, if you must go over there tonight, at least don't be pleasant. And if you can, play some sort of nasty trick on him."

Chandra glanced at her son, disturbed that he had heard any of this. "I'll do what I can for you, but I'm not playing any tricks on him! Now, please drop the subject."

Thirty minutes later, up in her room, Chandra stood staring into a long mirror. Before her was an image of a woman wearing a delicate ivory-lace camisole paired with a narrow clear-gold skirt. The image was of a sophisticated woman capable of handling anything. It was an image she had deliberately sought.

But Chandra couldn't see that image. Instead, in her mind's eye was a young girl in a crumpled aqua organdy dress walking home over a dark mesa, with tears streaming down her face, her sensitive heart hurting more than she had ever thought possible.

She told herself that she was being silly. Tomorrow Rick would call her and tell her he loved her and everything would be wonderful, just as she had dreamed for so long.

But day had followed day and Rick hadn't called. She spent long hours curled up in a tight ball on her window seat, withdrawing more and more into herself. And then she had seen an article in the local paper that to her mind had explained Rick's neglect of her. Rick's father had unexpectedly died of a heart attack. The funeral had been three days after their night on the mesa. Chandra felt better immediately. Now she understood. Soon, she was sure, Rick would call.

But he hadn't. Days had turned into weeks. Chandra had become more morose. Her body felt strange; her heart was filled with pain. Lillian, who knew nothing of what had happened, began to look worried.

Then one morning Chandra woke up to the fact she could no longer ignore. She was pregnant.

Chandra had never before known fear of any kind, but now she was scared, without any clear idea of what to do. Compulsively she read and reread her collection of articles about Rick. Finally she came to a decision. Since the death of Rick's father, it was obvious that he had been swamped with new responsibility. She would go to see him. As soon as she told him about the baby they were going to have, he would take her into his arms and make everything all right.

So she had dressed with care and driven downtown to the building where she knew his father had his offices. She could still remember how her fingers had shaken as she had run them over the newly painted letters that said Richard O'Neill on the office door. Inside, an expressionless secretary had told her that Mr. O'Neill's calendar was filled and perhaps another day would be better. But with screwed-up courage Chandra had insisted that she would wait. It must have been hours before the door to his office had opened and he had walked out with a group of men.

Her heart pounding, a tremulous smile pasted on her face, she had stood up. Without a break in his step he had walked right by her and out the door. Totally shattered, she had cried all the way home and had collapsed in Lillian's arms.

Lillian had put her to bed and called the doctor.

Later that evening Chandra had told her mother she was pregnant, leaving only the identity of the father a secret.

Lillian had been wonderful. Typically, she had said that, to hell with convention and what everyone thought, Chandra would stay in Monte Luna and have the baby. But Chandra wasn't as strong as her mother. She had insisted on going away, and in the end, for her daughter's sake, Lillian had given in and sent her to stay with her sister, Loraine, in Dallas.

Chandra reached out and touched the mirror's image. She had come a long way from that frightened, hurt young girl who fled Monte Luna nine years ago. She had finished her education, had survived a brief, broken marriage, and now held an interesting, satisfying job. There was no more pain or anger or fear left in her. Rick meant nothing to her anymore. He was merely someone she had to deal with because of Lillian.

After one final glance into the mirror, she picked up her purse and left the room.

They sat at a candlelit table on Rick's patio. Several feet away, the water of his swimming pool glowed aqua and translucent. A gentle breeze blew, stirring through Chandra's hair and bringing in the faint smell of sage off the plains. Absently she lifted her hand to pull a handful of her flaxen waves back. When she released them, they slid down with tousled order onto the golden skin of her shoulders.

Watching, Rick thought she looked like a goddess of the moon, golden and pale. *Chandra.* Lillian had done well in naming her daughter, for the name Chandra was from the Sanskrit, the name given to the moon, because it outshines the stars.

"Do you know a man named Nolan who's been doing odd jobs for Lillian?" she asked, taking a sip of wine.

He nodded. "He's a retired businessman. Came here about eight years ago and began farming peanuts on a small scale. He has a nice place west of your mother's."

"Is he one of the people who will have to move because of the lake?"

"No. As a matter of fact, his land will become lakefront property."

"So that's why he wants her to move."

"Everyone in town does, Chandra."

"So you told me." She looked up at him through a veil of dark lashes. "Do you have land that will edge the lake?"

He rested his forearms on the table and leaned forward. "Yes. A lot of people do. Unfortunately, Chandra, Lillian's property just happens to lie smack in the middle of a natural basin that has a nice-sized stream running right through it. With a dam on either end of that stream, the experts say the lake could be filled within six months, depending on the rainfall. If a good storm came along, it could fill in a week."

"I see."

"Do you? I hope so. We've been blessed with a lot of space out here in west Texas, Chandra, but water has always been a problem. In the past, droughts have paralyzed this area. Now our town is expanding and—"

Chandra held up her hand. "Pam's already told me most of this. And I do understand. What I don't understand is you."

He smiled. "I guess you remember me as a pretty wild kid, don't you?"

Her memories of him didn't bear thinking about, so she simply nodded.

"Well, you're right. I was. But when my father died, I inherited a great deal of responsibility."

"You were very young. You didn't have to accept it. Surely there were people who could have managed your interests until you were older."

"I never even considered it. You see, my father and I were very close. I thought the world of him, and he was so proud of me." He shook his head. "I'm afraid I let him down quite a lot. Yet he never indicated to me in any way that he was disappointed in me. Then early one morning I came home with a giant-sized hangover and found that he had had a heart attack in the middle of the night. It was a terrible shock to me. I had always seen him as invincible. It took me a long time to come to terms with the fact that he was actually gone and not coming back." His voice softened. "I felt I owed it to him not to let him down anymore. I just wish that he hadn't needed to die for me to grow up. I wish he could have lived to see what I've done for the town that he loved so much."

Chandra swallowed hard and looked away. She had been driven to ask him about that time right after their night on the mesa. Now she wished she hadn't. For years now she had thought that there was no excuse for the way he had ignored her afterward. She certainly didn't want to feel any compassion for him at this late date.

He leaned across the table and took her hand. "I'm sorry for going on about myself when we should be discussing your problem. You're in between a rock and a hard place, aren't you?"

She drew her hand from his so fast, she almost tipped over her wineglass. To her befuddled senses, his touch had seemed so hot, she was sure blisters would begin to rise on her skin at any moment.

She had pulled away from his touch again. Leaning back in his chair, Rick eyed her thoughtfully. "Who hurt you, Chandra?"

"I beg your pardon?"

"Who hurt you so badly, you can't stand to be touched? Was it your ex-husband?"

"Don?" she asked, startled. "Don never hurt anyone in his life."

"How long were you married?"

She reached for her wineglass. "A very short time." Suddenly she felt cold, and the wine sliding down her throat warmed her. "And it was my fault the marriage broke up"—*because I couldn't get you out of my system*—"so don't bother to psychoanalyze."

"Still, it must have been hard on Ty."

"Ty was very young when we parted. He barely remembers Don."

"He doesn't remember his own father? Doesn't he ever see him?"

She stood up and walked around the swimming pool to the waist-high fence, built to prevent anyone from wandering too close to the dangerous edge of the mesa. Below her the town spread like a carpet of lights. She felt Rick come up behind her, but didn't turn around.

"I'm sorry, Chandra, about whoever hurt you."

His words carried a gentleness that raised goose bumps on her arms, and in spite of herself she turned around and looked up at him. "It was a long time ago."

"But the effects are still with you, and it bothers me. I want very much to touch you without your pulling away from me. See . . ." His hand came out and stroked lightly down her hair to her shoulder. ". . . Like this. Feel? My touch isn't painful. I would never harm you. . . ."

She didn't pull away. She stood very still, barely able to breathe.

His hand brushed across her collarbone. "You're absolutely exquisite, and I want more than anything I can think of to see your glorious hair spread out on my pillow in the morning."

"Stop it," she said, but she whispered.

His fingers paused on the rapidly beating pulse at the base of her throat. His hazel eyes were very intense, very golden, but his touch was soft, careful. "I want you to get used to my touch, Chandra.

It tears something apart inside me when you pull away."

"Let me go," she said, although he wasn't holding her.

He lowered his eyes to the moistness of her lips, and then lower, to where his fingers covered the perfumed pulse point. "I want to kiss you over every inch of your body and have your golden skin melt beneath my lips." He lowered his lips to press against the place his fingers had touched. Slowly he inhaled, then raised his head. "I want to wrap myself in your allure—Chandra's Allure—from head to toe."

She was shaking. Her legs were weak. Her loins had begun to ache.

"Will you let me kiss you?" he asked in that soft, growly voice of his that was turning her insides to jelly. His lips were barely inches away from hers. His breath fanned warmly over her mouth.

She opened her lips to say no, but strangely, no sound would come out. Instead she heard herself moan. Then his lips closed over hers, and she knew she had been wrong about having no feelings left for him. As she opened her mouth wider to accept his exploring tongue, she admitted to herself that the emotions clamoring within her were both strong and real. Inside her, there might be residual anger and lingering pain—she wasn't sure. But she was in no doubt that there was also passion—stark, blazing-red passion—which threatened to override everything else. She pressed closer to him, feeling the heat from his body, savoring his exciting hardness against her.

Lord, she felt good in his arms, Rick thought as his hands roamed across her back and down to clasp her rounded bottom. He pulled her against him, cradling her pelvis against his, and a hot sweetness flowed into his veins like a narcotic. He wanted more. He couldn't imagine ever getting his fill of her. No woman had ever captivated him as much. Yet Chandra was strangely familiar to him. It was as if she had wound herself into him and were already a part of him. His reaction to her was a mystery to him, but one he had no inclination to delve into at that moment.

He kissed her face, her neck. He devoured her lips, and she responded as though she were on fire. The clothes that separated them became a frustration to him, so much so that his fingers found the buttons at the back of the camisole and began to undo them. It was perfectly clear to him that soon he would have her undressed and beneath him.

Her need for him had Chandra's head spinning, so that she had to admit to herself that she was a thread away from giving herself to him completely—just as on that night almost nine years ago, *that night when Ty had been conceived*.

No! Her need turned to panic. She could feel hysteria rising within her. With all her might she pushed against him, and succeeded in breaking away.

Rick held out his hands, bewildered. "Chandra . . . what is it?"

"Leave me alone!" she shouted. "Just leave me

alone!" And with that she grabbed her purse and began running toward the house.

He started after her. "Chandra, wait. Tell me what's wrong!"

Directly under a patio light she whirled to face him. Her hair fanned away from her head with a wild beauty, and her eyes glittered strangely. "Don't touch me! Don't come near me, not ever again!"

He let her go, not wanting to, but because he had to. Her shocking reaction to his lovemaking had cooled his passion as effectively as a shower of ice water, yet there was an ache inside him that remained. What had gone wrong? he asked himself, completely shaken. He grabbed his wineglass off the table and downed its contents in one gulp.

Had that been fear he saw in her eyes? Certainly there had been panic. But *why*?

"Damn it all!" he suddenly shouted at the top of his lungs. But no one heard. He felt totally helpless, and he hated the feeling. What should he do now? he wondered. He would never be able to leave her alone, he knew that. His feelings for her went far deeper than just wanting her—he didn't understand why; he just knew they did—which, of course, complicated an already complicated situation.

She was already a part of him. But if he felt that way, *why didn't she*? He took a deep breath. Lord, but he could still smell her perfume. It haunted him, like some fragile and elusive memory that wouldn't leave him alone.

He shook his head, trying to clear his mind. Whatever he decided to do, he would have to proceed with great caution. Whoever the bastard was who had hurt her, he had done an excellent job. How he would love to get his hands on the man for just five minutes.

Rick let his gaze sweep up to the night sky. He wished he could know if in some way her reaction tonight had been his fault. One thing he knew. He would never, ever want to do anything to cause that kind of reaction in her again. Seeing her that way had been like taking a hard blow to his solar plexus.

He unclasped his watch and laid it on the table, then quickly stripped his clothes off. As he walked to the edge of the swimming pool, he felt the cooling night air sweep over him. He savored the sensation for a moment, then dove cleanly into the water and began to swim lap after lap.

Morning light from the uncurtained window across from his bed struck against Rick's closed eyelids, slowly waking him. He yawned and stretched. Opening his eyes, he glanced at the clock. It was still early, but he had managed to get about four hours' sleep, all he really needed.

Sitting up, he stretched out an arm for his robe. The tempting smell of freshly brewed coffee reached him from the kitchen, and he silently gave thanks to the person who had invented the automatic coffee maker with a timer capable of being set beforehand.

Barefoot, he padded into the kitchen and poured himself a cup of coffee. During the numerous laps he had swum the night before, he hadn't been able to decide what he should do regarding Chandra. Yet he knew that he couldn't let matters stay as they were between them. He could no more stop himself from seeing Chandra again than he could fly to the moon.

With his coffee cup in his hand and a thoughtful expression on his face, he made his way through the house to the front door. Opening it, he stepped outside, intending to get the morning paper. But . . .

His bare feet sank into something sticky. He tried to step out of it, and started to slip. Quickly he grabbed a post to regain his balance. Looking down in confusion, he saw that his porch was covered with something clear and gooey. "What the hell?" Holding on to the post, he bent down and scooped up some of the substance on his finger. Gingerly he touched it to his tongue. *Corn syrup!*

Then he heard muffled laughter. Glancing around, he saw a small red-haired head sticking up from behind some shrubbery. In the space of time it took him to take four long strides, he was down off his porch and holding a struggling eight-year-old boy off the ground by his shirtfront.

"Ty Stuart, I presume?" Rick asked politely.

"Let me down! Let me down!"

"I'll be glad to. Just as soon as you tell me exactly what you had in mind when you decided to pour corn syrup all over my front porch."

Ty's face twisted defiantly. "Grandma says you're pond scum!"

"Really? And she told you to do this to my front porch?"

"She told my mom last night that she should play a nasty trick on you."

Rick lowered Ty to the ground. "And what did your mother say?"

"She said she wouldn't."

"So you thought you would. Okay, I have just one more question. How did you know this was my front porch?"

Ty crossed his arms across his chest to show he wasn't afraid. "My mom and Grandma were talking about where you lived. Grandma said one man doesn't need such a big place."

"I think you and I need to go talk to your grandmother. How did you get over here?"

Ty pointed toward his bike, stuck behind some shrubbery.

"Go get it, and we'll load it into my car."

Ty threw Rick a sullen expression, but he did as he was told.

Although Chandra was wide awake, she was reluctant to get up, because once she did, she was going to have to face some unpleasant realities, and she felt terrible enough as it was. She groaned and rolled over, burying her face in her pillow. Remembering how she had acted the night before made her burn with embarrassment. She had responded to Rick's lovemaking as if she had been starved for it, and then she had jerked away and screamed at him like some demented fishwife. She didn't know which made her feel worse. She still could recall the bewilderment on Rick's face, and no wonder!

She rolled over again and threw her arm over her head. Fortunately, she could think of no reason why she would have to see Rick again. As quickly as she could, she would make arrangements for Lillian to move, and then she and Ty would go home, back to their calm life in Shreveport.

The thought had her frowning.

Ordinarily a knock at the front door would have been heard only faintly in her room, since her bedroom was on the second floor and her door was shut. But someone had evidently taken that into account, because the pounding was loud enough to raise the dead. She jumped up and reached for her robe. She had heard Lillian go down to her studio about thirty minutes before, but as far as she knew, Ty was still asleep.

She raced down the stairs and opened the door. It took her a moment to realize that the scene in front of her was real, and not some nightmare. *Ty and Rick together?* And Rick barefoot and in a robe?

"Good morning, Chandra. I believe this child belongs to you."

Rick's arm was around Ty's shoulders, and Ty was looking none too happy. Her protective instincts leaping into play, Chandra reached for her son and drew him away from Rick. "What's going on here?"

"Ty decided to pay me an early-morning visit, didn't you, son?"

Chandra's heart nearly stopped beating when Rick called Ty "son." "I don't understand."

"Tell your mother," Rick prompted Ty.

"I poured corn syrup on his front porch," Ty mumbled, looking down at his tennis shoes.

"You what?"

"Evidently little pitchers have big ears, as the saying goes, and last night he heard Lillian call me pond scum."

"And des-pic-a-ble," Ty added with a spurt of spirit.

Chandra groaned. "Ty, how could you?"

The little boy shrugged, and resumed looking at his tennis shoes.

"Where did you get the syrup?"

"Out of Grandma's pantry."

"Did she know what you were going to do?"

"No, but last night she said—"

A light went on in her head. "But, Ty, that was no reason to do such a thing!"

"Ty, go get your bicycle out of my car," Rick said, "while I talk to your mom."

Ty hesitated, glancing up at Chandra. She nodded. Obviously greatly relieved to be out of the line of fire, he took off, quick as a jackrabbit.

Once Ty was out of earshot, Rick leaned one hand against the doorframe. The action raised his thigh-length robe even higher, to reveal strong, well-shaped thighs thickly covered with copper-tinted brown hair. "I'll forget this whole matter if

Ty will clean off my porch and you'll have dinner with me."

"Oh, look, I agree with you about having Ty clean off your porch. That's only right. But dinner? I mean, it was just a little prank."

"Really?" Rick sought to keep his gaze cool, but the sight of her standing there in nothing more than a thin, nearly transparent gown and robe had his blood surging. "I nearly slipped and fell, Chandra. Would you have called it just a little prank if I had broken my leg?"

"I . . . I'm sorry, Rick. I had no idea he would do such a thing."

"I believe you. So have dinner with me. I think we need to talk about what happened last night, don't you?"

She shook her head. "There's nothing to talk about. I'll admit that I overreacted, and I'll even apologize, if you want. But that's the end of it."

"I don't think so," he said softly. "I want to talk to you, and I think dinner would be the perfect opportunity. In fact, I insist."

"No."

"Well." He gazed around him consideringly. "I suppose, then, that I could call the sheriff out. There must be a law on the books somewhere regarding malicious mischief. Of course, we both know that the sheriff wouldn't do anything more than talk to the boy, but it would probably give Ty a good scare."

"You'd do that?"

"Are you going to have dinner with me tonight?"

"That's blackmail."

He grinned. "Do you know that you smell of your Allure when you wake up in the morning?"

"My what?"

"Chandra's Allure." His tone lowered. "I think you've worn it so long that it's a part of you. It's such an enticingly sensual smell, it stirs a man's emotions, making him want to absorb it and become a part of it too."

Suddenly realizing her robe had gaped open, she pulled it across her breasts and held it there. "Getting back to Ty, I'll have him come over and clean your porch off as soon as possible."

"Fine. And dinner?"

She let out a long breath. "Okay . . . but not at your house."

He nodded his agreement. "I'd prefer my home, but we'll do it your way. There are some nice places to eat in town now. I'll pick you up at seven."

"I'll meet you."

"No," he said quietly, but very firmly, "I'll pick you up at seven, and if you don't want Lillian to bring out the family shotgun again, I suggest you be on time."

Chandra sagged against the doorjamb and watched Rick stride toward his car. She waited until his car had driven off. Then she went inside to give Lillian a piece of her mind.

It was a few hours later that she looked out the kitchen window to see a tall, rawboned man striding in the direction of the barn. The man had to be Nolan, she decided, and headed out the door after him.

As she approached the barn, she recalled how, the day after she arrived, she had inspected the barn and found it in such excellent condition that Lillian was now using it for storage. She had given Ty permission to play in it, but Ty was now up in his room, grounded for the day. She didn't imagine he was suffering too much, though, not with his Transformers to keep him company and his grandmother sneaking treats up to him every so often.

The barn door stood open, and Chandra peered in, trying to see if the man was in there.

"Can I help you?"

She jumped in surprise and whirled around. He had come up on her so quietly, she hadn't heard him. "Are you Nolan?"

"Yes, ma'am."

It took her only moments to get a clear physical picture of Nolan. A worn cowboy hat covered most of his head, but she could still tell that his hair was steel gray and that his eyes were a clear gray. Signs of exposure to the elements were evident on his sun-darkened skin, which was understandable, since he was a farmer. He certainly didn't look menacing, she decided, and held out her hand. "I'm Chandra Stuart, Lillian's daughter. I've been wanting to meet you."

He extended his hand. "Nice to meet you."

He obviously wasn't a man to waste words, she thought, somewhat amused. "Lillian has told me how helpful you've been around here."

He nodded without speaking, and Chandra fought to hide a grin. She could see why Lillian didn't mind Nolan's being around. This man would go out of his way not to bother anyone. But that still didn't answer why he came by so often.

"I like what you've done around here, Nolan. Things look really nice. But considering that this property is going to be flooded soon, all your work will have been in vain."

"Yes'm, I guess you're right."

"Uh-huh." This one-way conversation was getting ridiculous. "I suppose, though, that you didn't know about the lake when you first started working here, did you?" she prompted.

"No, ma'am."

Enough was enough! she decided. "So, Nolan, why *did* you come to work here?"

He met her gaze directly. "I saw work that needed doin'."

"I see. Well, it's been nice talking with you, Nolan."

He touched the brim of his hat and disappeared into the barn, and Chandra was left shaking her head, because she knew no more about the man now than she had before she'd met him.

Four

Rick picked up Chandra and drove her to a very nice steak house on the outskirts of town. Halfway through the meal Chandra began to understand why Rick would have preferred to eat in the privacy of his own home rather than in a restaurant. He was a very popular man, and it seemed as though someone came up to say hello every few minutes. Chandra hadn't minded at first, but she found herself becoming annoyed.

She kept her gaze on her plate as she heard a man who had been introduced to her as Bob say good-bye and leave.

Rick turned back to her. "Sorry about that."

"It's all right."

"No, it's not." He paused. "Look at me, Chandra." She raised her head, and he smiled. "There, that's better."

"You're a very important man in this town, aren't you?"

"I suppose I am to the extent that I'm very involved in the town's future. I guess I just don't want to see it die away because of things like drought or the decline of the oil market. I'm concerned that the kids from this town, after they've been away to college or served in the armed forces, have something to come back to. I don't want us to lose good people."

She raised her water glass to her lips and took a sip. "I admire your dedication and your ideas. I wish you all the best."

"Do you mean that?"

"Of course."

"Tell me something, Chandra. Why did you leave Monte Luna so soon after your high school graduation?"

One by one her nerves began to coil tightly. "That was quite a few years ago, Rick. I was young, and I felt it was important at the time to leave here."

"And now? Is it still important to you that you stay away?"

She couldn't sustain eye contact with him. She looked back down at her plate, not even sure what was on it. "Yes."

"Chandra, is that you?"

She brought her head back up and encountered a pair of friendly dark eyes that she thought she remembered. "Yes, and you're Gloria, aren't you?"

The woman laughed. "That's right. It's so good

to see you back. I've been talking to Pam, and she tells me that she's throwing a barbeque for you in a few days. I can't wait."

Out of the corner of her eye she saw Rick signal for the check. "It should be a lot of fun. Do you know Rick?" she asked politely.

"Sure"—Gloria bestowed a beautiful smile on him—"although I wasn't aware that you two knew each other."

"Monte Luna is still a small town, Gloria," Rick said easily, having paid the waiter. He stood up and held out his hand to Chandra. "We look forward to seeing you at Pam and Robert's, but if you'll excuse us now, we're late for another engagement."

Gloria looked from one to the other with considerable interest. "Of course. As a matter of fact, I have someone waiting for me. It was nice seeing you again, Chandra."

"You, too, Gloria."

She waited until they were both seated in Rick's car before asking, "What other engagement?"

He slanted her a wry glance, then started the car. "Nothing to worry about. I just want to go someplace where we can talk uninterrupted."

Chandra remained quiet as Rick headed his car away from town. Settling back into the comfort of the beige leather seat, she listened to the wind and the road. But she wasn't soothed. She still could recall vividly a night much like this one, sitting next to Rick, speeding out of town.

But circumstances were different this time, she

reminded herself. Sitting beside Rick in the dark intimacy of his car now was rather like warming herself before a fire. She knew the fire possessed the ability to burn her, but she had no intention of getting any closer. She could be perfectly safe and still enjoy the titillation and the excitement of being close to a danger so attractive to her as Richard O'Neill. And it was heady to know that Rick, the man who had caused so much disturbance in her life, was attracted to her.

Mentally she shook herself. It was so unlike her to think this way! She had to be more cautious!

There had been a time when her heart would have palpitated wildly if he had merely tossed a careless smile her way. But he had broken her heart by using her, then forgetting her. She had a son because of him. She had a broken marriage because of him. The son had been worth all the pain. As for her broken marriage, Don, a completely innocent party, had had to suffer because of something that wasn't his fault.

Should she be thinking of extracting some kind of revenge, she wondered, instead of enjoying the way bubbles seemed to race through her bloodstream every time Rick spoke to her? Maybe so, but after all the time that had passed, and with Rick so close beside her, the place where black stopped and white started was beginning to blur in her mind.

While she was thinking, Rick had steered the car off the highway and onto a deserted country path. He pulled to a stop beneath a tree. Several yards away stood a large steel building. Lights attached to the roof flooded the surrounding area.

"What is this place?" she asked.

Rick pushed the seat back and turned to look at her. Chandra couldn't possibly know how she affected him, he decided, or she wouldn't be sitting there so calmly.

She was wearing a lightweight summer dress, part lace, part cotton, but it wasn't the dress that made her appear so damned beautiful and so impossibly romantic. Nor was it her flaxen hair, which rippled like waves of moonlight. It wasn't even her perfume, which hung lightly in the air, filling the car, teasing the edges of his mind, pulling at him. No, it was *her*, Chandra, and the completely natural allure that she had been born with.

He looked away from her, steeling himself for control. "This is a piece of land that I own. That building is a storage shed for various pieces of equipment. I thought we could find some privacy out here, along with some light. I wanted to be able to see you while we talked."

Caution returned to Chandra with a huge jolt. "Look, I went out to dinner with you in return for your agreement to forget what Ty did. Can't we just leave it at that?"

"No." His voice came to her as dark and soft as the breeze on which it was carried. "It's going to be a long time before I forget your reaction last night, but I'm hoping that maybe if I can understand it, I can fix it."

She propped her elbow on the door, leaned

her head against her raised hand, and looked straight ahead. "Some things simply can't be fixed, Rick. I've had to accept that in my life. It's time you did. Certain things are best forgotten."

He didn't take her advice. "You said it wasn't your ex-husband who hurt you. Is that right?"

"Don't probe, Rick."

"Then it follows there once was another man in your life besides your ex-husband. What did he do to you, Chandra, that makes you flinch so when I touch you?"

His soft voice hammered at her. "Nothing."

"I don't believe you. He must have done something. Who was he, Chandra, and what did he do to you to cause you to become nearly hysterical when you realized that in another moment we would be making love?"

A pulse began to pound hard in her temple. "Nothing."

"I still don't believe you. What did this man do to you that affected you to such an extent, you were unable to give yourself to me last night?"

No longer able to take the punishment of his probing words and his caressing voice, she whipped her head around so that she faced him. "He betrayed me! Okay? He *betrayed me.* Now are you happy?"

"No. Now I want you to tell me how long ago it was that he betrayed you."

"It was years ago, and it's over."

"Is it?"

She nodded. "I can't explain last night, any of it. All I know is that it would be best if you and I didn't see each other again after tonight."

He sighed heavily. "Chandra, I'm sorry, but what you're saying makes no sense at all. Now, on the one hand you say you're over whatever it was that happened between you and this man. And on the other, you say we shouldn't see each other again. I have to conclude you're really not over the man, whoever he was."

"You're wrong."

"Then prove it."

"What?"

"I said, prove it to me. Come here."

She sat there eyeing him through the dim light with all the wariness of a frightened animal, and Rick had to use every ounce of willpower he had, not to reach over and pull her to him. He wanted her in his arms so badly, his body pulsated with his need. He could feel the tension of his desire in every muscle. Yet he had to continue to go slowly. Chandra sat across the seat from him looking as delicate and as lovely as an angel might, but he could still remember the way, for that all-too-brief period of time the evening before, she had nearly dissolved in his arms from the fire between them. He wanted her like that again.

Chandra could feel her breasts rising and falling rapidly with the increased rhythm of her breathing. Her nipples had grown hard and were jutting through the fine cloth of her dress. And all because Rick had asked her to slide across the seat and into his arms. The whole situation would have been ridiculous if it hadn't seemed so ironic. He was asking her to prove she was over him . . . by making love to him. . . .

And she was very much afraid she was going to do it.

She just wasn't sure why. It could be, she decided, that by crossing the short space separating them, she could prove to herself she was indeed over him. Or it could be, simply, that she wanted to.

Slowly she inched toward him, until her thigh touched the knee he had propped up on the seat. Without taking his eyes off her, he dropped his knee off the seat, and she shifted across the remaining space.

Rick had one arm resting on the steering wheel; his other arm lay along the back of the seat. Because he made no move to touch her, Chandra gingerly placed her hand on his chest. Beneath her palm she could feel the thud of his heart. Its slow, steady beat somehow reassured her.

She skimmed her hand across his chest to the open collar of his shirt. There her fingers encountered a thin layer of hair, and beneath the hair, warm skin. She wanted to touch him.

Raising her head, she found his gaze locked with hers, and it was telling her to explore as much as she wanted. There had been so many years when she had wanted to do just that, the temptation was almost irresistible.

One by one she undid the buttons on his shirt, then spread it open. Dropping her eyes to his chest, she took a deep breath at the sight. Wonderingly she ran her hand across the expanse of silky hair to the smooth skin at his side. Next she moved it over to first one flat nub, then the other. Her own breasts began to ache as she circled the smooth skin around his nipples.

Beneath her fingers she could feel his heartbeat accelerate and turn to pounding. Glancing up into his eyes, she again found encouragement. He was silently conveying that she could do as she wanted. And she realized there was something she wanted to do rather badly, something she had never done before. With one last look at him, she lowered her mouth to one of his nipples.

She heard his breath catch as her tongue tentatively circled the hard tip, then flicked across it. Her hands were splayed on his chest, and she could feel his powerful reaction to what she was doing. It was a strange kind of high to have him in her power. Maybe this was a type of revenge in itself, but she was relishing it. Carefully, experimentally, she took the nub between her teeth. Rick groaned.

Lifting her head, she saw that the gold-green of his eyes appeared brilliantly colored, his lips were parted, and his breathing was labored.

She placed her hand on his neck, angling it so that her palm rested on the rougher skin of his neck and her fingers curled upward into his hair. She stroked her other hand across his jawline until her fingertips played along his lips.

"Chandra." Her name came out of his mouth as

a low, soft growl that affected every single one of her senses. "Kiss me."

He was asking; he wasn't telling. The air from the opened windows fanned her, cooling her. But inside she was burning.

She leaned forward until her breasts rested against his bare chest. The material of her dress was so thin that she could feel the brush of the hairs on his chest through the fabric. She pressed her breasts harder against him, and heard a strange, painful sound escape his lips. She couldn't stand it any longer. Twining her arms around his neck, she began to kiss him.

Her tongue darted between his lips, then back out again. When he didn't respond, she plunged her tongue back into the wet, warm cavern and found it suddenly entwined with his.

Then his arms were around her and he had taken over. But not in a way that frightened her. She was in exactly the position where she wanted to be. She had known what she was doing, and she had no one to blame but herself. The kiss continued as their bodies strained together.

Rick pulled her closer into him, while fighting to keep one part of his mind clear. He knew he had to stop their lovemaking soon, but Lord, it was going to be hard. He had never held a more passionate woman in his arms. Whether she knew it or not, he could have taken her right then on the seat of his car and she wouldn't have uttered a protest. And his body was screaming at him to do so.

But it was afterward that he was concerned

about. He was thirty-one years old, and there had been a lot of women in and out of his life, with varying degrees of involvement. Yet something inside him had always stopped just short of commitment.

With Chandra he felt no such reservation. In fact, he wanted to bind her to him with anything and everything he had, and once he made love to her he was convinced she would never get away from him again.

But he was still aware of the need to go slowly. When it happened he wanted it to be absolutely right between them. So gradually he pulled back from her. He felt the sweetness of her breath on his face as she sighed deeply.

Gently he brushed her hair back from her face, then cupped her cheek. Her skin felt hot to the touch, and he had to steel himself so that she wouldn't feel the quiver that ran through him.

Her eyes were clouded by her passion. He couldn't help himself. He kissed her again, gently, softly.

"Rick?"

"It's time I took you home." She looked at him uncomprehendingly. "I don't want to," he murmured, "but if I don't, you may regret it in the morning, and I don't want that." He stroked his hand down her cheek to the smoothness of her neck and encircled her throat with his hand. "Thank you, Chandra."

"For what?"

"I needed to hold you in my arms tonight and kiss you without your flinching or becoming frightened. You gave that to me."

For some reason that Chandra couldn't comprehend, her eyes filled with tears.

Smiling tenderly, with his fingertip he wiped away a solitary tear that had spilled down her cheek. "There's no need for tears, because it's going to happen between us. Not tonight, but soon. It's your decision, Chandra, and I'll wait."

The smell of turpentine and oil paints filled Lillian's studio. Paint-splattered and jar-lined worktables sat against two walls. The other two walls were glass, allowing the light to enter that Lillian needed for her painting. She stood in the center of the room before a tall, old-fashioned easel, critically studying the canvas in front of her, which was filled with the bold splashes of color and strong, sure lines that were her trademark.

"We'll be gone only a couple of hours," Chandra was telling her. "Can I pick up anything for you?"

"You might get something for dinner," Lillian murmured absently, then swiveled around with a frown. "Did you tell me where you were going?"

Chandra sighed. "Yes, I did. I want to buy Ty some boots. His sneakers just aren't providing him with the protection he needs here, walking around the farm."

Ty skipped into the room. "I'm ready, Mom. Grandma, I'm going to get some real cowboy boots!"

Lillian's usually austere face dissolved into a tender smile. "That's what I hear." She cast a glance at her daughter as she weighed some ideas.

"Offhand I can't think where to tell you to buy his size boots."

"That's okay. Pam told me that O'Neill's Department Store carries the best selection for kids."

"*O'Neill's!* Don't you dare go there!"

"Lillian, if that's where I have to go to get Ty his boots, then that's where I'll go."

"Surely there's someplace else. You shouldn't give that Richard O'Neill one cent of your money!"

Chandra took Ty's hand in hers. "We're going now, Lillian. See you when we get back."

Pam had been right about the selection of boots. Twenty minutes in O'Neill's had been all the time Chandra and Ty needed to purchase a pair of boots they were both satisfied with. And as they explored, they discovered that O'Neill's offered an equally impressive selection of clothing, jewelry, appliances, video and stereo equipment, and just about anything else a big-city department store might have.

She left Ty browsing in the toy department, sporting his brand-new pair of boots, while she selected a new dress for Pam and Robert's party. As a fashion buyer, she was an expert in women's clothes, and it took her no time at all to find exactly what she was looking for. In the end, she chose two dresses.

While she wandered back to the area where she had dropped off Ty, Chandra studied the layout of the store with a professional eye. Try as she might, she could find nothing to fault. Although she would have done a few of the displays with a bit more flair, all the merchandise was laid out with an eye to attractiveness and easy accessibility.

She was peering into a jewelry case, admiring a gold filigree necklace, when she felt a tap on her arm. Wheeling around, she confronted a strange man.

"Excuse me, ma'am. Are you Ms. Stuart?"

"Yes, I am."

"Would you come with me, please? It concerns your son."

"Ty! What's wrong? Is he hurt? What's happened?"

"He's not hurt, ma'am. He's up in Mr. O'Neill's office."

She felt the blood drain from her face. "Richard O'Neill?" she asked, although she really didn't need verbal verification.

The man nodded and turned to lead the way toward a set of elevators. Chandra followed, her heart pounding. She had expected to see Rick again, of course, but not quite so soon. After last night she needed time to recover, she told herself, then wondered if there was that much time in the world. During the hours before dawn, her dreams had been filled to overflowing with him, and she had awakened confused and mortified that her longing for him was so intense, it had penetrated to her subconscious.

Chandra had never had an affair of any sort, but this morning she had awakened actually wondering if she could be capable of having an affair with Rick, and at the end of it be able to go back to Shreveport and resume her life. It staggered her that she was even *thinking* about it, but nevertheless she continued to do so. With little over a week left of her vacation time, the affair would have to be brief, of course. If they had an affair. *If*.

And available time wasn't the only reason the affair would have to be kept brief. There was Ty. She had no idea what would happen if Rick were to discover Ty was his son, and she had no desire to find out. The decision that the two of them, father and son, must be kept apart had been a natural one on her part.

But now this man, whoever he was, was telling her Ty was with Rick.

It turned out that the fourth floor of O'Neill's consisted of business offices, not only for the department store, but for Rick's other interests. His own office took up a large portion of one corner of the building. The strange man ushered her in, and took up a position behind her.

Chandra's gaze slid over Rick and went right to her son. She didn't like what she saw. Ty was looking very defiant, but she knew him well enough to realize that he was on the verge of tears. She started toward him, but the grave tone of Rick's voice as he softly said her name checked her.

Her gaze flicked to Rick, then questioningly back to Ty. "What are you doing up here, honey? I thought you were going to wait in the toy department until I came for you."

Ty folded his arms across his chest and looked down at the tips of his shiny new boots.

"Chandra," Rick began, "Ty was caught shoplifting by Mr. Swanson." He nodded toward the man behind her.

"*Shoplifting!* Oh, no, you're wrong! There's some mistake. Ty would never do anything like that." Quickly she crossed to her son and put her arm around his shoulders to hug him reassuringly. She glanced behind her to the silent Mr. Swanson. "Who are you, anyway?"

Rick was the one who spoke. "He's a security officer here at the store, and I'm afraid there's no mistake. Ty was caught out in the parking lot with this tucked inside his shirt." He picked up a small figure of a Transformer from his desk, and Chandra recognized it immediately as one that Ty had been wanting.

Behind her Mr. Swanson cleared his throat. "I saw him take the toy, but I didn't stop him until he was outside. That's store policy."

Rick nodded at the man. "Thank you. That'll be all."

He waited until the three of them were alone, then said gently, "Why don't you sit down, Chandra? You, too, Ty."

Because her legs felt as if they were about to give out on her, Chandra took his advice and motioned for Ty to do the same.

Looking at their pale faces, Rick mentally cursed the situation. But because he was a man who faced things head on, he knew there was nothing for it but to continue. "Evidently, Chandra, Ty's plan was to stash the toy in the backseat of your car, then return to the store and wait for you, as you had told him to."

Her disbelief that Ty could have done such a thing was fading, but her deep love for her son and loyalty toward him made her ask, "Is that right, Ty?"

Ty's red head was bowed, his hands clenched tightly in his lap.

"Ty, answer me please."

There was a pause, and then he nodded.

Chandra's hand came up to massage her brow.

Rick felt her pain and wished that he could have spared her this. But for the boy's sake he knew he was doing the right thing.

One large hand waved across his desk to the Transformer. "Tell your mother and me, Ty, why you took this."

"I wanted it," Ty mumbled.

"But, honey, I thought we had agreed that you were going to save up your allowance. You must have known you would get that one sooner or later. You have nearly the whole collection as it is." When Ty remained silent, she turned to Rick. "I don't know what to say. He's never done anything like this before."

He smiled at her, wishing he could go to her, take her in his arms, and erase that stricken look from her face. "I believe you. But at the same time I don't think we can let this go by as easily as we did the corn-syrup incident, do you?"

She sank back in her chair and shook her head, knowing Rick was right. Ty had to be punished.

Like most single parents, she had her guilts and concerns over whether she was in any way shortchanging Ty, raising him alone. Now all her inadequacies as a parent, both imagined and real, washed over her, nearly making her sick to her stomach.

Rick switched his gaze to Ty and regarded him thoughtfully. "Was there some other reason you took the toy, Ty . . . besides the fact that you just wanted it, I mean?"

Chandra placed a hand on her son's shoulder. "Answer Mr. O'Neill."

Ty's blue eyes shone earnestly at his mother. "It was what Grandma said."

"What did Grandma say?"

"She said that Mr. O'Neill shouldn't be given a cent of our money."

Chandra groaned, and Rick fought to hide a smile.

Resting his forearms on his desk, Rick leaned forward to address the boy. "If you don't know it yet, Ty, you should learn now that there are two sides to every story. In this case, your grandma's side and my side. Before making a judgment on any subject, you should know both sides. Always remember that." His gaze went to Chandra, then back to Ty. "So what sort of punishment do you think you ought to get?"

For the first time since he had walked into Rick's office, Ty became anxious to talk. His small face turned hopeful. "I'll never do it again. I promise."

Rick nodded, his face serious. "I'd like to think you won't, but you see, that's not how the law works."

Ty gulped, his eyes big. "Law?"

"Stealing is a crime, Ty, and it's a crime that always carries a punishment." Rick threw a quick glance at Chandra to see how she was holding up, and was relieved to see color had returned to her face. Still, she wore a worried look that tore at him. "You know, I have quite a few flower beds at home that need weeding. If you were to come over tomorrow afternoon and weed them for me, I think we could call this settled."

Ty wrinkled his nose. "Weed?"

Chandra took hold of Ty's arm and pulled him to his feet. "He'll be there," she said, giving her son a grim look. "And, young man, I also want you to apologize. Now."

Ty hung his head. "I'm sorry."

"And so am I, Rick," she said, and received another smile from him that made her wish for things that couldn't be. "We'll leave you to get back to your work."

Rick caught Chandra's elbow as she was about to follow her son out the door. "Don't worry," he said, low, so that only she could hear, and gentle, to soothe her overworked nerves. "Ty isn't about to become a juvenile delinquent. He's just a little boy who's caught up in a situation he can't understand."

"Like a lot of people, I guess," she murmured, gazing up into his hazel eyes and deciding she had never seen them more beautiful.

"Like a lot of people," he repeated softly, and let her go.

Rick's comment to her about Ty came back to her on the drive home, and she turned it over and over in her mind, feeling warm. Rick couldn't possibly realize how important his simple words had been to her.

Circumstances and time had seen to it that he would never know Ty was his son, but she supposed some portion of her must have wanted, needed, his reassurance that she was doing a good job raising their child. Because his understanding of Ty's problem meant more to her than she would have thought possible.

Five

Lillian, of course, had been furious that her grandson was going to be forced by that cruel Richard O'Neill to weed his flower beds. She had let Chandra know her feelings about the matter in no uncertain terms, using the colorful and inventive language that she resorted to on those occasions when she was upset over something she felt had hurt either Chandra or Ty. But she had related her views in private, as Chandra had forbidden her to say anything at all to or in front of Ty.

Now, driving toward Rick's home to pick up Ty, Chandra wondered how her son had fared during the afternoon. When she had dropped him off four hours earlier, he had been a tense, pale little boy with a mutinous look in his eyes and a sullen expression on his face. She had had to fight against all her protective, motherly instincts in order not to get out of the car and stay with him.

Chandra steered her car under the arch and into the long drive that led up to the big house. Scanning the front of the house, she could see no sign of either Ty or Rick. That was odd, she mused.

A short time later, her finger on the doorbell failed to bring any response. Perplexed, she gazed around her and finally decided to walk toward the rear of the house.

As she drew closer, she heard loud splashes of water, and shrieks of laughter that she recognized as Ty's. Not knowing what to expect, she hurried around the corner of the house, stepped onto the patio, then stopped.

In the pool, Ty and Rick were frolicking like two playful porpoises. Prepared for tears and an unhappy son, Chandra could hardly credit the scene in front of her.

Ty looked up and saw her. "Mom! Hi!"

Rick ducked his head under water and surfaced with his copper-brown hair slicked back out of his eyes and gleaming with a wet luster that appeared red in the sunlight. He smiled and waved. Bewildered, she returned the wave.

"Mom, come in and swim with us. We're having a great time!"

Aware of Rick's warm gaze taking in the briefness of her shorts and halter top, she crossed the patio. "So I see." At the edge of the pool, she knelt down and addressed her son. "Did you finish all your weeding?"

"Oh, yeah, a long time ago. Rick helped me."

Chandra couldn't get over Ty's remarkable change of attitude. Her attention switched to Rick, and she raised her eyebrows in silent question at him. "He did?"

Playfully Ty swept his hand across the surface of the water, sending up a spray. "And you know what else?"

"No, what?"

"Rick said he admired me, 'cause I'm loyal to you and Grandma and I try to take care of you."

For a brief moment Rick's eyes locked with hers, yet those moments were long enough to make her heart miss a couple of beats. Swallowing a lump in her throat, Chandra smiled at her son, then at Rick. "That was a nice thing for you to say to him. Thank you."

"I meant it." Rick swam over to the edge, and in one lithe movement levered himself onto the deck. Water sluiced off his body in streams that trailed each curve and hard muscle of his torso until finally abandoning his beautifully formed shape to pool around his feet.

Her eyes took the same path as the water, and encountered a sporty bikini that rode low on his hips. Her experience as a buyer told her the black swimsuit was made of Lycra spandex. Her instincts as a woman informed her that ninety-eight percent of his body was still bare. Trying not to look, but doing so anyway, she corrected herself. Maybe that figure should be ninety-nine percent, and the remaining one percent might as well have been exposed, too, for his impressive manhood was clearly outlined, and she was left in no doubt as to the potential of his virility.

All at once her chest tightened as she remembered that Rick had once been inside her. She had never thought her imagination to be particularly good, but now it seemed to her that she could actually feel Rick between her thighs.

"Well?" Rick prompted, enjoying the flush that was currently creeping up Chandra's throat to her face.

She started. "W-well what?"

"Are you going to come in and swim with us?"

"I—I can't. I don't have a swimsuit."

She gestured to her attire, and his gaze followed . . . to the short shorts that curved over her hips and stopped high up on her long legs . . . then to the halter that cupped her luscious round breasts. He hadn't held her breasts in his hands yet, but the need that pounded through him told him that he would have to soon or go mad. The fact that he could hear Ty splashing happily away behind him should have cooled his ardor, but it didn't. In a minute he was going to embarrass both her and him. "You don't need a swimsuit. What you have on is fine. Ty is swimming in his shorts."

"I know, but that's different."

"I don't think so," he said mildly. Then, before she knew what he was going to do, he grabbed her by the shoulders and fell sideways with her into the pool. Spitting water, she surfaced to the cheers of Ty. She swished around, looking for

Rick, and found him across the pool, treading water beside Ty. "You two are going to pay!" she yelled, and started after them. And so the playing began.

It was some time later, exhausted, that she leaned her back against the side of the pool and rested her head on the deck behind her. Down in the shallow end of the pool, Rick was teaching Ty how to toss a quarter into the water and retrieve it.

Letting her legs float weightlessly, she tilted her face up to the sun and closed her eyes, thinking, *this shouldn't be happening.* Ty, Rick, me . . . it's dangerous . . . the potential for heartbreak and disaster is enormous . . . I've spent nine years avoiding this very thing . . . *but it seems so natural!*

Water lapped against her, and she opened her eyes to find Rick directly in front of her. Bracing his feet on the bottom of the pool, he put his hands on either side of her head and pressed his body full length against hers, causing her floating legs to spread, so that the back of her upper thighs rested on the tops of his.

"Having fun?" he asked.

She nodded, glancing over his shoulder toward Ty, who, engrossed in his game, was paying no attention to them.

With one hand he grasped her bottom and settled her more firmly against his pelvis. She could feel his hardness between her legs now, and something inside her began to dissolve.

"I like being here with you this way," he murmured. "With your clothes plastered against you." He slid his hand from her bottom, up her side, until it rested just under her breast. Feeling the heavy beat of her heart against his hand, he knew he could wait no longer. He eased his fingers beneath the halter, and because the back of the garment was elasticized, it gave, and he was able to lift it to bare one breast.

She gasped and looked again for Ty. In the shallowest end of the pool he was trying to learn handstands. It occurred to her briefly that one of the advantages of Ty's being an only child was that he was perfectly content to play by himself. Or was that a disadvantage?

Rick's hand was now completely filled with her breast, and compulsively Chandra wrapped her legs around his back, even while she gasped out, "You shouldn't do this."

"It's all right," he whispered. "I'm shielding you. He can't see anything. He's too far away. To him it just looks like we're talking."

"What *are* we doing?"

He tilted his pelvis into hers. "We're loving." His mouth came down to cover a spot at the base of her neck, and his finger teased and pulled at her nipple. Chandra bit her lip to keep from crying out her passion. For a brief moment he released her breast, and beneath the water he pulled the front of his swimsuit partway down. "I love being with you here," he repeated, beginning a sensuous rhythm with his hips so that, with every other heartbeat, his sex, naked and hard, was pressed high up between her thighs. "But the chlorine has washed away the scent of your perfume. I miss it. And I wish you didn't have on shorts."

She was wishing the same thing. "You're doing pretty well, considering," she somehow managed to get out.

He chuckled. "And I don't like the fact that I can't bend my head and take this"—two fingers closed over her nipple—"into my mouth and find out what it tastes like."

This time a low moan, full of her longing, escaped her lips before she could stop it.

Rick shuddered. "I want you, Chandra. I want you so much, I don't think I can stand living through one more day without having you. Right now all I can think of is how easy it would be to pull down your shorts and enter you. Do you have any idea how it would feel?"

"No . . . no . . . no . . ." The denial came from the conscious part of her mind, but her subconscious was impelling her to move her hips against him.

His fingers were now at the leg of her shorts, sliding upward. . . .

"Mom! Rick! Watch me. I've learned how to stand on my hands underwater."

Rick didn't remove his hand, but he did glance over his shoulder. "We'll watch." As Ty dove underwater, Rick's finger slid under the elastic of her panties to her softness.

The pleasure was so intense, Chandra's body jerked.

"Did you see that?" Ty yelled.

"We sure did," Rick called. "That was great. Show us how many times you can do it." Ty enthusiastically plunged back underwater, and Rick turned eyes almost pure gold back to her, marveling that he had been able to call to Ty, because when he looked at Chandra his throat became so tight, he could barely speak. "Tomorrow night . . . the party . . . bring your swimsuit and we'll come back here afterward and swim."

She shook her head.

"Yes," he whispered. "Just you and me. Alone. Alone, Chandra!" His mouth came down and covered hers with a kiss that conveyed the depth of his passion for her. Between her legs, against the seam of her shorts, she could feel his enormous need. "Yes!"

"Mom! Rick! I stood on my hands seven times. Did you see?"

Rick lifted his head and stared into her eyes. "Well?"

She drew in a shuddering breath. "Maybe."

He reached for the front of his briefs and pulled them up. "You'd better go on over to Ty. I've got to wait a few minutes."

Chandra was amazed that the water around them was not boiling. She knew her face was flaming. Casting Rick one last, helpless glance, she struck out to swim to her son.

Ty bolted from the car as soon as Chandra pulled to a stop in front of Lillian's house. Chandra looked after him, perplexed. He had been unusually quiet on the drive home. Chandra followed her son into the house and caught up with him in Lillian's studio, where she found him with his arms clasped tightly around his grandmother's waist and his face buried in her stomach.

Lillian, for her part, was definitely in ill humor. "Chandra! What in the world did that man do to my grandson?"

"If by that man you mean Richard O'Neill, he did nothing other than, let's hope, help Ty learn a lesson that stealing is wrong and then showed him a good time."

"Good time! What do you mean, good time? And why is his hair wet? Ty, honey"—she held him away from her—"what's wrong? Talk to Grandma."

He stood back, but refused to look at either her or Chandra, instead gazing down at the floor.

Her heart pumping overtime with worry, Chandra walked over to him and laid her hand on her son's shoulder. Could it be that he was upset because he had somehow been able to see what she and Rick were doing? No, that was impossible, she told herself. He had been too far away from them, and besides, Rick's body had shielded her. "His hair is wet because after he finished weeding— which, by the way, Rick helped him do—the two of them went swimming. When I arrived to pick him up, he was having a great time."

Ty quickly looked up at his grandmother. "Yeah, but I didn't have a lot of fun, honest, Grandma. I didn't."

Chandra's sigh of relief was so great, she was afraid it had been audible. So that was it. Ty was afraid that by actually having fun with Rick, he had been in some way disloyal to his grandmother. She went down on her knees and took her son in her arms. "Ty, it's all right that you had fun, really, it is. Grandma's problem with Rick is not yours, and you shouldn't feel that it is. The two of them will solve it by themselves, and soon, too." She pulled back and looked into Ty's wide blue eyes. "I'm sure Grandma appreciates your support, but I know she doesn't want you to be unhappy." She switched her gaze to her mother. "Do you?"

Lillian's forehead was pleated in a frown of consternation. "No. Goodness, no! Ty, honey, come here." Ty went back into his grandmother's arms and hugged her tightly. "All I want in the world is for you to be happy, and if you had a good time today, then I'm glad."

He peered up at her. "Really?"

Lillian stroked his hair. "Really. I'm only sorry that you had to weed Richard O'Neill's flower bed because of something you did for me."

"Aw, it wasn't so bad."

"Good. Then why don't you go wash the chlorine out of your hair, and I'll make you something special for dinner."

"Great!" Ty's face lit in a great big smile of happiness that included them both, before he ran out of the room.

When he had gone, Chandra turned sternly on

her mother. "This has got to stop! I will not have Ty torn in two like this."

Lillian sighed. "I know. I just didn't realize."

"Well, now you do. And one more thing. You've got to face your situation realistically, Lillian. You've got to understand that this is one fight you're going to lose."

"Now, that's where you're wrong. The town is going to have to give in, because I have no intention of moving."

In exasperation Chandra ran her hand through her hair, and realized that she, too, had better go wash out the chlorine. She threw her mother a last glance, a glance that held sadness mixed with love. "I wish I could make you understand how wrong you are, but I can't seem to. So be it. I just hope you'll come to your senses before it's too late."

Colored hurricane lights circled the wide patio. Music from a local band drifted on the night air. At one end of the patio there was a long table arrayed with an inviting and plentiful selection of food. Set up at the other end was a well-stocked bar. Small tables with pale pink tablecloths dotted the rim of the area. Somewhere along the way, Pam had learned how to throw a successful party, Chandra thought. Everyone seemed to be having a marvelous time.

Except her. Her nerves were on edge. Part of the reason was that Lillian, whom Chandra had never in a million years thought would come to the party, had decided to grace them with her presence. Of course she would come, she had said. The party was for her daughter, wasn't it? But Chandra knew her mother, and she was very much afraid Lillian might create a scene. Currently Lillian was holding court in a circle of admirers, at her regal best, wearing a stunning Chinese blue silk blouse and long skirt that had come as a total surprise to Chandra, because they were so unlike the attire her mother usually wore.

Off to one side, Nolan stood. Tonight he was spruced up in dress pants, a western shirt, and a string tie. It was interesting, Chandra mused, how he watched Lillian without appearing to, and she again wondered at his motives.

Through the crowd she saw Rick bend his head to a woman, listen, then smile at what she had said. A stab of jealousy pierced Chandra's heart, followed swiftly by resentment. Here she was, a grown woman, still feeling the emotions she had known as a foolish teenager. Back then she had also watched Rick talk and laugh with other girls.

But there was a difference now, she reminded herself. Tonight he was with her. And *he* was the main reason her nerves felt raw.

In a few hours the party would be over, and they would go back to his house. What then?

She hadn't intended to bring her swimsuit, but when Rick had arrived at Lillian's to pick her up, he had threatened to make a scene that would bring both Lillian and Ty out of their rooms. She had given in, running upstairs and snatching an old bikini out of the drawer. His eyes had revealed his satisfaction when she descended the stairs with the suit in a bag. They had also revealed a heat that had made her shiver with its promise.

"Why aren't you mingling?" Pam demanded, appearing at her elbow.

"I have been. I just thought I'd take a breather. Rick has gone to get me something to drink."

Pam's face split into an approving smile. "Things sure seem to be going well between the two of you. Who would believe you met only six days ago?"

Neatly sidestepping her friend's curiosity, Chandra turned to her. "Pam, this is a wonderful party. I can't thank you enough."

"It was my pleasure. I love to entertain, and I know I won't be able to do much for a while after Junior is born." Pam patted her belly. "Boy, do I envy you your flat stomach. I can't even remember the last time I saw my toes. That's a dream of a dress, by the way. That shade of peach makes your skin look golden."

Chandra laughed, running her hand over the sheer chiffon of the halter-neck dress. "Thanks. I like it too."

"You know, tomorrow I think I'm going to go out and buy me a knockout of a dress in a size eight. It will give me something to look forward to." Pam's gaze roamed over the crowd, seeking out any sign of trouble. Unerringly her gaze stopped at Lillian. "I'm so glad your mother is here tonight. Her presence has insured that I'll have the most talked-about party of the year. I don't know if you're aware of it, Chandra, but she rarely leaves the farm anymore. She even has her groceries delivered. She was always reclusive to a certain extent, but after you moved away she withdrew totally."

"Really? I had no idea." Chandra absorbed this bit of information with a troubled expression. "I'll definitely talk to her and see what I can do. In the meantime I just hope she behaves herself tonight. Who is that earnest-looking young man she's talking with?"

"The mayor. Don't worry. He won't say anything to upset her—he's too much in awe of her."

Chandra chuckled. "It's not *him* I'm worried about."

Rick, suddenly at Chandra's side, slid his arm lightly about her waist and handed her a drink. "Having a good time?" he asked, bending so that he could see her face.

Because Pam was beside her, she nodded. In truth, she wished she were up in the bedroom she had had as a young girl, sitting in the window seat, spinning dreams. Dreams that didn't come true couldn't hurt.

She had dreamed once of her and Rick's being a couple. For one short night they had been. He didn't remember that night, and she'd been trying to forget it ever since it had happened. But now it seemed they were a couple again. Yet once more it would be for only a short while. Would she spend the rest of her life trying to forget this time too? she wondered.

Pam muttered a mild expletive. "Beth Phillips has got Robert cornered. "I'd better go rescue him." As she hurried away, she threw parting instructions over her shoulder at Chandra. "Mingle! Mingle! This is your party, after all. These people are here to see *you*."

Chandra laughed. "We'd better do what the lady says."

"Not yet," Rick murmured. "First I want to spend some time holding you." He set their drinks aside and led her to the dance floor that had been laid on the patio.

The band was good, and there were quite a few other couples dancing to the slowly pulsing beat of the music. But Chandra was soon wishing that they were alone, for the moment Rick pulled her against him, a thrill of longing shot through her, so intense that her legs almost gave way beneath her.

"Have I told you how beautiful you look tonight?" he asked, his mouth at her ear.

"I—I can't remember."

His low laughter sounded in her ear, and the effects of it curled in the pit of her stomach. "Then I must not have told you." With a subtle movement he shifted his sports coat aside, so that her breasts and his chest were separated by only the chiffon of her dress and the cotton of his shirt. She felt his hand brush across the bare skin of her back. "I like this dress."

Talk about the mundane, she told herself. "I got it at O'Neill's. You have a really excellent dress department." Her ploy didn't work.

"I want to leave right now," he murmured. "I want to lift you into my arms and carry you out of here."

"We—we can't leave."

"I know you want to, though. Your nipples are hard. I can feel them, and it is exciting me beyond belief."

It was exciting her too. "Stop it!" she whispered.

"I can't, and I don't want to. I don't care if everyone here knows how much I want you."

In a minute she was going to be lost in the maelstrom of her own passion, she thought helplessly. "Rick . . . these people . . . they're watching."

"No one's watching."

A quick, surreptitious glance around told her Rick was right. But it didn't help her situation any. She was still in danger of succumbing to a yearning so deep, she was beginning not to care that they were surrounded by people.

He nuzzled his face into her neck and inhaled deeply. "Your perfume disturbs me on an impossibly deep level. I wake up in the middle of the night, thinking that I can smell it. It's haunting and evocative, just like you, capable of driving me quietly out of my mind."

Humor saved her. She laughed softly up at him. "As long as it's quietly."

He grinned and pulled her more tightly against him.

Over his shoulder, her eyes met the sharp-eyed gaze of her mother. Hastily she broke away from him. "Rick, we've got to mingle."

He nodded. "Okay, okay . . . for now."

She and Rick made their way from group to group, dutifully speaking to everyone. Surprisingly, names and faces came together easily for Chandra, and she found herself enjoying seeing old friends and acquaintances. Although she knew it couldn't be true, to her they all appeared to be untouched by time, while she felt absolutely pulverized by it.

Rick pulled her to a halt in front of a trim, gray-haired lady. "Chandra, I'd like you to meet Shirley Brown. Shirley is in charge of the buyers for O'Neill's."

"It's nice to meet you," Chandra said sincerely. "I visited the store the day before yesterday and admired your displays."

"Thank you. And it's nice to learn that our efforts are appreciated. Rick tells me you're a buyer."

"That's right. In Shreveport."

"And do you enjoy it?"

"Very much." Because Shirley seemed to be interested, Chandra briefly told the older woman of her experience and training.

When Chandra was through, Shirley nodded admiringly. "Around here, a qualified buyer is hard to come by. We sure could use you. Any chance of your coming back here to live?"

Flattered, she nevertheless said, "None."

Rick leaned down and whispered, "Would a firm offer help change your mind?"

Her eyes rose to his in astonishment. "You're behind this!"

"You can't blame a guy for trying."

"The offer was genuine, Chandra," Shirley said. "Rick may be my boss, but I would never hire anyone who wasn't qualified. If you change your mind, let me know. I, for one, hope you decide to stay."

"Me too," she heard Rick murmur before leading her off to talk with another group.

Although Rick hadn't asked directly, the knowledge that he wanted her to stay in Monte Luna enough to offer her a job gave her a warm glow. But she gave herself credit for not reading more into his gesture than there was. If she had changed, so had Rick. She knew that now. He was a genuinely nice man. Maybe beneath all that wildness nine years before, he had even been a nice boy. Circumstances had prevented her from finding out.

Rick's "Good evening" startled her back to the present, and she glanced up to see that he was speaking to her mother. Holding Chandra's elbow, Rick nodded to Lillian. "It's good to see you here this evening."

Chandra wondered how they had gotten to Lillian's group without her being aware of it, then realized that for the past hour Rick had been gently steering her toward her mother. Two by two, the people who had been standing around Lillian discreetly dispersed.

Lillian leveled steady blue eyes on Rick. "I was about to leave. I've had my fill of everyone here tonight telling me how wonderful you are."

The corners of Rick's mouth twitched. "And you, of course, didn't believe them."

"Not a word."

"Well, then, why leave? Just ignore them and have a good time."

Lillian fixed him with her most intimidating stare. "Why are you trying to drown me, young man?"

Rick, however, was not intimidated. In fact, when he spoke, Chandra could hear the deep vein of humor that ran through his words. "I'm a great admirer of yours, Lillian. I have quite a few of your paintings hanging in my home."

"Really?"

"Really. And I would never, under any circumstances, no matter what the provocation, try to drown you."

"Yet, if you have your way, my property will soon be at the bottom of a lake. If that's not trying to drown me, I don't know what is."

"It's progress," he said. "And I believe you understand that. You're too intelligent a woman not to."

"Buttering me up isn't going to work, you know."

From somewhere to Chandra's side she heard someone snort softly, "Stubborn woman." She turned and saw Nolan. Then she heard Lillian say something else that she wished she hadn't heard.

"And neither will dating my daughter!"

Rick's arm went around Chandra and drew

her close, as if to reassure her of the sincerity of his words. "Dating Chandra and the lake project are two entirely different matters," Rick stated flatly. "They're not to be confused in anyone's mind."

Lillian's gaze went thoughtfully to Chandra, then back to Rick. If she really puts her mind to it, Chandra thought, Lillian will figure it all out—everything about Rick, her, and Ty.

"You know," Lillian said, "I've never really understood why Chandra insists on siding with you over me."

This conversation should be ended immediately, Chandra decided. "Lillian, it's not a matter of sides! It's a matter of your not having any options. You're going to have to move."

Lillian shrugged and pulled out a cigarette. "I don't agree with you, but let's say for argument's sake that you're right. Where would I go?"

Rick produced a folder of matches from his pocket, leaned forward, and lit the cigarette. "With the money you're going to earn on the sale of your property, you could buy a nice piece of lakefront property with a view."

"View!" Lillian sniffed her disdain. "There is no view to compare with what I have now. And what about the house I've lived in all my adult life?"

"If you're that attached to the house, it can be moved," he answered calmly.

"Moved?" Scorn underscored the one word. "Not my house!"

"Then I'm very much afraid you're going to have

to resign yourself to the fact that it will soon be under fifty feet of water."

"And to hell with heritage, right?"

"I beg your pardon?"

"Heritage—the land on which I now live has been in Chandra's family for generations, and my plan is to pass that land on to my grandson."

"Your grandson is a fine boy, Lillian. I've grown extremely fond of Ty. But I think that if you asked him what he would want most for you, he would say your happiness. Whether it's been consciously or unconsciously, you've transmitted your unhappiness to him, and he's reacted."

Lillian's indignation seemed to cause her to grow several inches in front of their eyes. "And you felt obligated to punish him."

"I did what I thought was right."

"Which is all I'm doing."

Rick's gaze switched to Chandra, and she was relieved to see that his eyes were twinkling. "Have you ever won an argument with your mother?" he asked her.

Lillian didn't give her a chance to answer. "Yes! When she decided to leave town, it was completely against my wishes." Her tone was disgusted and disgruntled. "And what's more, I haven't been able to change her mind."

"Well, then, we have more in common than you think, because we're in total agreement on that particular subject."

Suddenly no one had ever had more of Lillian's attention than Rick did at this moment. It seemed to Chandra that her mother was about to say something, but then changed her mind. "I think I'm ready to go home."

"Do you need a ride?" Chandra asked.

"No, I came with Nolan." She looked around her as if she had lost something "Oh, there you are, Nolan."

Chandra's surprised gaze went to the silent man.

Lillian raised her eyebrows at her daughter. "I assume you'll be home early."

"Well, I—"

"Actually, she won't," Rick cut in smoothly. "We have plans for after the party. I wouldn't wait up, if I were you. Tell Ty his mom will see him in the morning, and that I'll be over too."

Six

"And this is the bathroom," Rick said, throwing an absent glance around the room where black lacquer, marble, and bronze abounded, and everywhere there were mirrors, plants, and, most of all, luxury. There was a Roman-style tub, as well as a steam bath and Jacuzzi.

"If I had a room like this, I doubt if I'd ever leave it," Chandra said sincerely, but lightly, trying to fight the tension she could feel accelerating between them by the minute now that they were finally alone.

He grinned. "There are some days I don't want to, believe me." He pointed toward two doors. "That door leads to a workout room, and behind the other is my wardrobe. Why don't you go back out to the bedroom, and I'll get my suit and collect a towel for you."

She nodded, grateful to leave the intimate, sensual atmosphere of the room. But the bedroom wasn't much better. Silk-walled and thick-carpeted, the enormous room seemed to be dominated by the large four-poster bed—if not in actual fact, at least in Chandra's mind. Clutching to her chest the bag that contained her swimsuit, she stood staring dumbly at the bed, every doubt she had ever had suddenly inundating her.

Searching for a place that wouldn't worsen the state of her rapidly deteriorating nerves, she made her way into the sitting area that was just off the bedroom. She had caught only a brief glance of it before, but now she studied it, trying to see Rick here. It was a charming place, a perfect spot for reading and relaxing, and she wondered if Rick ever took advantage of it.

A wall of cabinets and shelves drew her closer. As she might have expected, there were plenty of books. But the small teddy bear with the tattered fur she wouldn't have expected. He was propped up against a picture of Rick's father in a sterling-silver frame. Then there was an old, well-used baseball mitt lying alongside a scuffed leather football, very likely the first baseball mitt and football Rick had ever had. She ran a finger across the rough leather of the football, trying to see in her mind Rick as a young boy, learning how to throw it. Ty had a football similar to this one, she realized, but it wasn't real leather, and he didn't have a father to teach him how to throw it.

Her attention switched to an elaborately detailed model of an old sailing ship that took up most of one shelf. She couldn't imagine the hours of patient work it had required to put such an intricate model together.

"My dad and I did that together."

"Oh!" Chandra jumped. Because her concentration had been so intense, she hadn't heard Rick come up behind her, but now she turned to him. "You mean you actually built it? How long did it take you?"

"Longer than it should, I'm afraid. We worked on it on and off for a couple of years, mainly during the winter months. But I can still remember the day we finished it. You've never seen two happier people."

There was a special look Rick got whenever he talked about his father, and it touched her. "You miss him, don't you?"

He nodded. "Anything good that I've become has been because of him. He was a busy man, an important man, but he always had time for me. If I'm ever lucky enough to have a child, I know I'll be a good father because of the example I had."

Chandra's heart lurched, painfully, fearfully, perhaps even a bit guiltily. She shouldn't be here, she thought. She was about to tell him she was leaving, when he spoke again.

"Chandra, I owe you an apology."

She could hear the unique softness in his voice that he used when he talked to her, as if he had to be extraordinarily careful of her. Once she would have been in heaven at that tone. Now it only served to confuse and disturb her. "An apology?" She felt his hands lightly grip her upper arms.

"Yes. I'm rushing you. I'm putting all kinds of pressure on you, when I know that I shouldn't be. And I'm sorry." Slowly he swiveled her around to face him "But you see, I know you'll be leaving here in about a week's time, and I'm beginning to panic."

She licked her lips nervously. "There's no reason to. We've had a good time, but—"

His grip tightened. "Don't *do* that! Don't try to minimize what has happened between us." He paused and, as he had gotten into the habit of doing, lifted his hand to brush her hair gently back from her face. "And Chandra . . . don't be nervous. Tonight, it'll be enough for me just to be alone with you. Nothing else has to happen if you don't want it to. I promise you I won't be upset." He gave a low laugh. "I may be uncomfortable as hell, but not upset. Okay?"

She nodded, unsure of what she wanted to say.

He gave her a brief hug, then released her. "There are a couple of towels on the bed. I'll change in another room and meet you out at the pool."

A few minutes later Chandra was casting a dubious look at herself in the mirror, doubting whether she would have the nerve to appear before Rick in the suit.

The bikini had once been violet, but years and use had faded it until it was almost lavender. The suit was cut modestly by today's standards, she reflected, twisting this way and that, trying to tell herself she looked all right. She seemed to remember wearing the suit with complete ease when she was a teenager. But her body was fuller now;

her hips were rounder. Frowning, she ran a hand over her stomach. Was it as flat as it had once been? she wondered. And her hair! Clicking her tongue in disgust, she combed her fingers through the shining mass. It was just as unruly as ever, waving with unrelenting abandon down her back to just past her shoulder blades.

Oh, hell! Angry with herself for even caring what Rick thought, she jerked up a towel and headed for the door. It just didn't matter, she told herself. After all, they were only going to swim.

With her hand on the doorknob she halted. It was time to stop fooling herself. They were going to do more than swim. Much more. It was true that Rick had left the decision up to her, but she realized now that she had made the decision, almost without even being aware of the thought processes involved.

Later there would be regrets, she was sure, but she was a grown woman now. Life had taught her a lot of hard lessons, and she had of necessity been a good student. She had learned that kisses don't mean promises, and that lovemaking doesn't guarantee a happily-ever-after ending.

Rick wanted her, and she wanted him. From that first contact with him at the gas station, her body had reacted to him with a remarkable memory of its own. And his interest had certainly been obvious enough.

She didn't regard what was going to happen between them tonight as an affair, but rather as a continuation of something that had been started ten years ago. Only this time there would be a proper ending. Instead of running away, she would walk away, her head held high.

With that resolved, Chandra opened the door and left the room.

The patio and pool area were empty when she arrived, with no sign of Rick. Grateful for the respite, she dove cleanly into the water and began swimming laps. She didn't count how many times she swam the length of the pool and back again. But before she reached the outside edge of tiredness, and with her body feeling refreshed from the exercise, she reached blindly for the side and surfaced, her flaxen hair streaming sleek and wet down her back.

Rick was there, sitting with his legs dangling in the water. Without a word he slipped into the water beside her.

"How long have you been there?"

"A while." He reached out a fingertip to wipe away water drops that clung to her lashes. "I was enjoying watching you. You're a very good swimmer."

"I don't get to do as much as I'd like, but I do try to take Ty in the summertime to the public pools. He learned to swim at the Y. He's very good for his age, don't you think?"

He smiled at her, and the tender understanding in his smile nearly undid her. "Why are you talking so much?"

She tried to laugh, but found she couldn't. "Because I'm nervous."

"I told you, there's no need. Unless . . ." He looked into her eyes, and unwaveringly she returned his gaze. What he saw there must have given him his answer, because he drew in a deep, hard breath.

She dropped her eyes, only to notice that water had darkened the hair that grew across his chest. Almost unaware that she was doing it, she lifted her hand to the silky wetness. "Rick, I—I haven't been with many men."

"How many?"

"There was my husband . . . and one other man."

"The man who hurt you."

She nodded, fighting to control her breathlessness.

"I'm going to erase him from your mind," he whispered, leaning down to kiss the wet, cool skin at the base of her throat. He inhaled deeply and knew a momentary disappointment that the chlorine had washed away her perfume. But then he took another breath and smelled woman, a sexual, mysterious fragrance that he found to be even more potent than the perfume that had been created expressly for her. "After tonight you won't be able even to remember his name."

She might have laughed, except Rick chose that moment to untie the top of her swimsuit, and it floated away.

Resting the back of his head against the ledge of the pool, he let the water raise his weightless body so that he reclined on the surface. Then he pulled her on top of him, and the exquisite brush of her hardened nipples against his bare chest sent flames licking through his veins. "Chandra," he murmured, "I can't even begin to tell you how much I want you."

With both hands cupped around the back of her head, he pulled her face toward him and kissed her long and hard. The motion sent water gently lapping against their bodies.

Intense heat flooded through Chandra, until she felt fused to him. A rushing sound filled her ears. Wrapping her arms tightly around his neck, she returned his kiss with a fervor she hadn't known she possessed.

Rick moved one hand up and down her spine, learning the indentations with his fingertips. The water had turned the feel of her skin to satin. Beneath her soft body he was hard, aching with a need that by the minute was getting more and more difficult to restrain.

Slipping his hand beneath the bottom of her swimsuit, he caressed the curve of her buttocks, kneading the soft flesh, then pressed downward with his palm so that she could feel how desperate his need for her was. She reacted by wrapping her legs around him, and he wondered if he was going to be able to wait.

But he had to wait, he reminded himself. This night must be as good for her as he knew it was going to be for him.

He slid his hands over her body, then up under her arms, and lifted her out of the water until his lips were even with her breasts. Taking a nipple into his mouth, he sucked, tasting water and sweet, sweet Chandra.

Above him, he heard her cry out. "Do you want to go inside?" he asked huskily.

"Oh, yes, yes. Rick, take me inside."

He did, carrying her in his arms, not willing to break the contact they had established in the pool. Once in his bedroom, he lowered her feet to the floor. They had left their towels outside, but neither cared.

Rick stripped off his trunks, watching while Chandra slipped out of the bottom half of her suit. Soon they were lying entwined together on the ivory suede spread that covered his bed, and her body was quivering beneath his with a restless, pulsing energy.

He tried to hold back, but it was no use. He couldn't get inside her fast enough or deep enough to satisfy him, and she seemed to feel the same. She arched up to him, receiving him with a welcome that tore any remaining sanity from his mind.

Together they were wild, together they were right, together they broke through the boundaries of reality and soared.

Her long hair was still wet, her skin pearlized with the dampness caused by the exertion of their lovemaking. Lying close beside her, Rick stroked his fingers through her hair, gently, patiently, separating the strands, combing the tangles out, until the flaxen length lay in an undulating glory around her head.

When he had finished to his satisfaction with her hair, he gazed down into her face. "I've known you in my dreams, Chandra," he murmured, his voice carrying a passion-soft huskiness. "Somehow, in some way, we are linked."

Slowly she opened her eyes, and what he saw there shocked him. *Wariness.* Her old wariness was back, and he had no idea why. He barely resisted the urge to utter a string of violent oaths.

"What do you mean?" she asked.

He rested his hand beneath her left breast so that he could feel the beat of her heart. "Nothing at all sinister." Rubbing his hand back and forth under her breast, he whispered, "Tell me about the man who hurt you." Even beneath his moving palm, he felt her heart jolt.

"Why?"

"Because I can tell that our making love didn't cause you to forget him." His hazel eyes, more green than gold at the moment, showed a strange hurt.

"Did it make you forget your previous lovers?"

He answered her defiant question with a simple response. "Yes." She tried to roll away from him, but he wouldn't let her. Firmly he brought her back to his side. "Tell me."

Chandra met the intensity of his gaze, felt the caress of his hand that, even now, was making gentle circles on her stomach, and knew that if she lived to be a hundred and ten she would never be able to forget him.

"The man who hurt you is Ty's father, isn't he?" he prompted. "That's the reason your ex-husband never sees Ty, and the reason Ty doesn't seem to remember very much about your ex-husband. Chandra, answer me. *Is that it?*"

Painfully, the answer erupted out of her. "*Yes!* Okay? Yes!"

Rick flung himself back on the pillows with an oath, and curiously Chandra discovered she wanted to comfort him. She raised up on an elbow. Much as he had done, she laid her hand over his heart. Beneath her palm, she could feel the heavy beat that signified his anger, his strength, even his passion. "It's all right, Rick. It was a long time ago. I don't hurt anymore. Ty and I have done very well on our own."

He gave a self-depreciating chuckle. "I know you've done well, but I still find myself wishing you hadn't."

His statement puzzled her. "Why?"

"Because"—he turned to look at her—"I want you to need me as much as I need you. Marry me, Chandra."

"What?" Her breath rushed out of her with a force that was caused by her total astonishment.

Now he was on top of her, supporting most of his weight on his elbows, holding her face between his two large hands. "Marry me. Spend the rest of your life with me. Let me be the father Ty has never had. Let me be the lover who will satisfy you so totally that you will never want another."

Speechless, she could only stare at him.

"Do you have any idea how beautiful you are?" he whispered, moved by the confusion and vulnerability he saw in her eyes. "Do you have any idea how much you affect me?"

He moved against her then, and she felt the still-hard, potent evidence of his need. Nudging at the softness between her thighs, he sent a thousand nerve endings quivering to life. His hand closed around her breast, gently kneading her flesh with enough care not to hurt her, but with enough pressure to show the building of his feverish desire. His mouth came down open on her lips, his tongue driving inside.

And Chandra felt the world begin to slip away.

Her legs were already spread, and Rick could wait no longer. He thrust into her. A shudder ran up and down his spine as he felt her muscles contract around him. "I love you," he said.

She heard him, and her mind registered what he said. But she couldn't react, because her body was being taken over by his. It was possession of the most erotic kind. And so Chandra surrendered to it, because she could do nothing else, and because, at this moment, there was nothing more important.

"Did you hear me?" Rick asked. "I said I loved you." Minutes earlier Chandra had gotten out of bed, and wrapped his robe around her as she eyed the chair where she'd left her clothes the night before. She was now standing at the dresser, trying to bring order to her hair.

Without looking at him she said, "Yes, I heard."

It was at times like this that he wished he smoked, Rick mused dryly. He had never before told a woman he loved her, and now that he had, the woman was ignoring him. He supposed he deserved it, after all the women he had bedded, then left. Still, he couldn't help but wish that Chandra were back in bed with him and he were holding her close. At least then he would have some control over the situation.

"Chandra, come here."

She lifted her eyes to meet his in the mirror, but she made no move toward him.

"Please come here."

Slowly she walked to the bed and took a perch on the edge.

"I want to tell you something," he said softly. "All my life I've been searching for one woman, who up until now has only been in my dreams. When you came to town, my dream became reality."

Chandra dropped her head to stare at the comb in her hands. "Don't say that."

He sat up in bed, unconcerned that the sheet no longer covered his nakedness. With a finger under her chin, he turned her head toward him. In her eyes he saw the confusion and the wariness, but there was something else too. Could it be pain? His brows drew together in a frown. "Chandra, I don't understand what's wrong. To me it all seems so simple. You and I together are magic. I want you. I want your child. I want us to spend a lifetime together. I've asked you to marry me."

She swallowed hard, and it drew his attention to her long, creamy throat. "I know," she said softly, "and I'm really—"

"Don't you *dare* say you're honored! Dammit, Chandra, I won't let you say no to me!"

She bolted off the bed, and a sound came out of her throat that might have been a laugh, except to his ears there was too much pain in it. But the expression she turned on him was resistant, almost angry. "This town might do everything you say, but I don't live in this town anymore. I can say no if I want to."

"But don't!" In a movement that combined strength and grace, he came off the bed to stand in front of her. Deliberately speaking quietly, he said, "Chandra, I'm a straightforward man. Believe me when I tell you that if I could change the past and your hurt, I would. I can't, though. It's impossible." He lifted his hand to the side of her neck and stroked its length. "But what I can do is cherish you for the rest of your life and protect you from all hurt."

"No!" Chandra pushed away from him and took a few hurried steps. Only when there was a safe distance between them did she turn to him. "Rick, I'm sorry that you can't seem to accept my refusal of your proposal. Nevertheless my refusal stands. I can't marry you, and since I probably couldn't explain my reasons well enough for you to understand them, you're just going to have to accept it."

She scooped up her clothes and rushed into the bathroom. Almost slamming the door, she closed it and turned the lock, then leaned back against it, trembling.

What was she going to do? she asked herself despairingly. She felt as if she might come apart, important bits and pieces of herself flying away, never to be recovered.

Most of the major decisions and events of her life had been dictated by her feelings for Richard

O'Neill. There had been a time when her day would have been made just by the sight of his smile. Then that night on the mesa had happened. And she had run, a scared young girl. The problem was, she was still running, and she didn't seem to know how to stop!

A week ago, when she drove into town, she had thought she had her life together. But she had encountered Rick and history had begun to repeat itself—only in a much more real, much more vivid way than she had ever thought possible. Even now, with a locked door between them, her body was still glowing from his lovemaking and was clamoring for more.

But that was her body. In her mind the past was still too strong. The past had dictated her adult life. She had had a child because of the past. She had married a nice young man and moved from Dallas to Shreveport because she'd hoped she would be able to forget Rick. Because it hadn't worked, she had divorced that nice young man. She had stayed away from Monte Luna because of Rick. *When,* she asked herself in genuine anguish, *was she going to stop making decisions based on Rick?*

And now they had made love. She had walked into his arms with her eyes wide open. Or had she? Could she ever really be totally rational when it came to Rick?

Groaning, she pushed away from the door. She had never felt more unbalanced in her life. Her mind was in a turmoil, split in two. Fool! The romantic side of her said. Rick had just offered her what she had wanted ever since she was sixteen. But the rational side cautioned, Slow down! Loving Rick was a dream of her youth. She'd had one bad marriage. Did she really want another? Was she really in love with Rick or was she in love with a dream of her past?

She let the robe slide to the floor and padded to the glass-enclosed shower. Turning on the water full blast, she stepped in. Her body was redolent of Rick and his lovemaking, and she reached for the soap to wash his scent away. But it wasn't that easy, because the soap was Rick's soap, and instead of scrubbing his scent off, she was washing it on. Clean, healthy, spicy . . . sexy. She closed her eyes and inhaled. God, she wanted nothing more than to return to the bedroom and climb back into bed with him.

But determinedly she made herself go through the motions of showering, and afterward she didn't linger. She put on her clothes as quickly as she could manage and went back out to Rick, to find that he, too, had dressed.

"Drive me home, please."

He nodded. "If that's what you want. But, Chandra, I'm not giving up."

"Rick"—she lifted her hand toward him, but then dropped it when she realized what she was doing—"try to understand. I need distance and time to give me a perspective on this. I think it would be a good idea if we didn't see each other for a while."

"A while?" His voice was raised incredulously. "Chandra, you're leaving town in seven days." He paused, and his eyes took on a speculative gleam. "Unless . . ."

"Unless what?"

"I'll make you a deal. I won't ask you to marry me again, if . . . if you'll stay here."

She started to shake her head.

"Think about it, Chandra. Lillian would love to have you here. I'd even go so far as to say that she needs you, now more than ever. She's got a lot of difficult decisions to make, a lot of adjustments ahead of her."

Her heart sank, because she knew he was absolutely right. The knowledge made her angry. "That's not fair. What about me and what I need?"

"You have friends here. I'm here. It would be one of the easiest things you've ever done, making a new life here."

"I have a job waiting for me."

"And you have one here, if you want it. At O'Neill's."

"It's impossible. Ty—"

"Would adapt easily. Kids do, you know."

He was capable of defeating her so easily, she thought with despair. With just a bit more effort on his part, he could sway her and make her do what he wanted, especially now when her mind was split in two and her thoughts were scrambled. But she couldn't allow that to happen. "Please take me home, Rick."

Seven

In front of Lillian's house Rick switched off the engine of his car. Immediately Chandra groped for the door handle, but Rick's hand closed over hers. "I'll come around and open the door for you."

At his touch, her skin came alive with need. She stared out the window, refusing to look at him for fear he'd see the desire that his nearness evoked. "That's not necessary."

"Yes, it is. And I'm also coming into the house with you."

Her head whipped around so fast, her hair lashed against his face. "I told you, I want us to stop seeing each other."

"I know—for a while."

"That's right." She glanced toward the house. "Besides, it's early. No one's up yet."

"Then I'll start breakfast for everyone."

"Rick, didn't you listen to me back at your house?"

He was still leaning toward her, so that it took very little effort for him to lift his hand and trace her bottom lip with his finger. "Oh, I listened. I listened to your moans. and I listened to you saying, 'There, Rick, touch me there,' and 'Don't stop, Rick, please don't stop.' "

A flush started at the base of Chandra's neck and climbed to her face. "That's not what I meant, and you know it!"

Slowly he smiled. "Do I? Well, in any case, there isn't any point at all in arguing, because you see, Chandra, I have a problem."

She got careless, giving in to the urge to lower her eyes to his smiling lips. "Problem?"

He nodded. "I will give you anything in the world I can, I will acquiesce to your wishes until I am dust in the ground, but, Chandra . . . I can't, I won't, go even a day without seeing you."

Her mouth opened, but words didn't seem to come.

He dropped a kiss on her open mouth. "Now I'll come around and open your door for you."

Having changed out of her peach chiffon dress into jeans and a tank top, Chandra sat sipping a cup of freshly perked coffee and observing Rick narrowly. Currently whisking a bowl of eggs to a froth, he was also overseeing a pan of bacon sizzling near his elbow. Her skepticism over Rick's abilities in the kitchen were fast disappearing, but her belief that it would be better all around if they didn't see each other again still remained strong.

"Mom?"

She jerked around at the sound of Ty's sleepy voice. "Good morning, honey." She held out her arms, and he went into them for a hug. Still in his pajamas, he was warm and soft from sleep.

"Hi, Rick," Ty murmured bashfully, peeking out from his mother's arms.

"Hi, yourself, sleepyhead. I hope you like your eggs scrambled."

"What are you doing?"

Rick laughed. "What does it look like I'm doing? I'm cooking breakfast."

Ty ventured closer to the stove and stood on his tiptoes so he could get a better look. "Really? I've never seen a man cook before."

Rick's expression softened, but his tone was teasing. "Well, it would appear that you have a lot to learn. These are hard times for men. We've got to be able to look after ourselves. I'll tell you what. Come over here, and you can help me cook the eggs."

"Honest?"

"Sure." Rick poured the eggs into an already hot skillet and handed Ty a spatula. "Just start stirring, and in no time at all you'll have a pan of light, fluffy eggs."

"Wow!"

Rick met Chandra's gaze and winked.

This is dangerous, she thought. Rick and Ty

together is *so* dangerous. By some miraculous stroke of luck, Ty's coloring had fallen in a range that was somewhere between hers and Rick's, and there was no obvious resemblance between the two of them. Still, how long would it be before people started seeing what she saw—a certain turn of the head, a similarity in the slant of the nose, father and son?

"What's going on here?"

Chandra jumped at Lillian's sudden entrance into the kitchen. Lord, she thought, at this rate her nerves would soon snap completely.

For his part, Ty dropped the spatula and took several steps away from the stove.

Only Rick remained calm. "Good morning, Lillian. You look as if you could use a cup of coffee. Ty, are you deserting your duties as cook here?"

Ty looked at his grandmother, then at his mother. Chandra nodded encouragingly at him.

"No," he said, and went back to his position at the stove.

Lillian helped herself to some coffee and added cream and sugar before going to join Chandra at the table. Taking several sips, she viewed her daughter over the rim of the cup. "I gather you've just gotten home?"

Rick had been checking on the progress of a pan of biscuits, but suddenly he straightened and slammed the oven door shut. "Lillian! Wasn't that a great party last night?"

Her eyes narrowed on him, but as her grandson was standing beside him, she nodded. "Very nice."

"It looked like you were having a great time.

Nolan brought you, huh?" He paused politely, but since Lillian didn't say anything, he continued. "Great guy, Nolan. Has he taken you out to his place yet?"

Lillian's face contorted with indignation. "Nolan is my handyman. Of course I haven't been out to his place!"

Chandra was growing more alarmed by the minute at the exchange between her mother and Rick, and she tried to signal him to take it easy.

He ignored her. "Don't get me wrong. I wasn't suggesting that anything improper was going on between you and Nolan, but—"

Lillian half rose out of her chair. "*Improper!*"

"Are these eggs done?" Ty asked.

"They look great, son. Here, I'll take over now. You did a first-class job, by the way." Rick held the skillet at an angle. "Look at the wonderful eggs your grandson cooked, Lillian."

The sharpness of Lillian's gaze should have cut Rick in two, but to her grandson she said, "Terrific job, Ty."

Rick laid his hand on Ty's shoulder. "Why don't you go get out of those pajamas and wash your face and hands? The rest of the breakfast should be ready by then."

"Okay." Ty beamed happily and skipped out of the room.

Lillian lit a cigarette. "Now, suppose you tell me, Richard O'Neill, what you're doing here, when you know you're the last person on earth I'd want in my home."

He bent to retrieve the baked biscuits out of the

oven. "I wanted to spend some more time with Chandra, and I thought it would be a good opportunity for us to talk."

"I have nothing to say to you."

"Maybe not, but I have some things to say to you."

Chandra, unable to sit still, hopped up and began setting the table. "I think it would be a good idea if nobody said anything," she muttered.

Lillian exhaled heavily, and squinted at Rick through the veil of smoke. "What was all that about Nolan?"

"Nolan is a good man. He has a wonderful place, well run, well maintained, not too far from here. I just thought you might have been interested enough to go and see it."

"Interested enough?"

"How long has it been, Lillian, since you've looked and really seen anything but your own farm?"

She reached for another cigarette. "I have no idea what you are talking about."

"Neither do I," Chandra mumbled.

"You're an amazing woman, Lillian, with a God-given talent. A lot of people come out here to west Texas, and they're unable to see the beauty of it. But you look and see a grace in the ruggedness of the land, a symmetry in a stand of mesquite trees against a wide blue sky, a purpose in a rutted dirt road, and you paint it so that everyone else can see it too."

Chandra looked anxiously at her mother. Lillian was always uncomfortable talking with anyone about her painting. There was no telling what she would do.

Lillian puffed furiously on her cigarette. "If you have a point to make, young man, then I suggest you make it, because, as I've told you before, buttering me up is going to do you no good at all."

Rick handed Chandra a plate of bacon to set on the table. "I don't regard the stating of facts as buttering anyone up. And my point is, I think you're missing a good thing by holding so fiercely to this property."

Chandra inhaled sharply. "Rick, I think you'd better go."

Rick eyed Lillian steadily. "Unless I'm very much mistaken, you haven't painted anything for years that wasn't drawn from either something you can see out of one of these windows or a place within easy walking distance of this house. Tell me I'm wrong."

Lillian's smile was definitely not to be trusted. "Ah, but you see, young man, that's the beauty of sitting in my own kitchen. I don't have to tell you a damn thing I don't want to."

"What is it, Lillian? Are you afraid that if you have to leave here, your talent will dry up?"

Lillian placed a fresh, unlit cigarette between her lips. "My daughter's absolutely correct, Mr. O'Neill. It's time for you to go."

"Is Rick right?" Chandra asked, surprised. "Are you afraid you won't be able to paint if you move somewhere else?"

"Of course he's not right!" Lillian snapped.

Ty burst through the door. "Is it ready yet? I'm starved!"

"Sit down, Ty," Rick said, "and I'll get you a glass of orange juice. We can hardly wait to eat those eggs of yours."

"Me either!" Ty took a seat beside his grandmother and looked around with interest.

Chandra gave up and sat down too. There was no sense in her worrying about either her mother or Rick. They were two strong-willed people who were perfectly capable of taking care of themselves. Still, it was interesting that Rick seemed to have hit a nerve with Lillian about her painting. Chandra poured herself another cup of coffee and sat back to see what would happen next.

Rick filled Ty's plate with bacon, eggs, and a biscuit, then served Chandra.

Ty took a tentative bite of his eggs, then another. "Hey! These are good! Have some of my eggs, Grandma."

"I'm not hungry," she said, glaring at Rick, who had just dished a nice portion of eggs onto her plate.

Chandra reached over and shoved the plate a little closer to her mother. "But because Ty cooked them, you will try them, won't you, Lillian?"

Lillian fixed a smile on her face. "I can hardly wait."

A knock on the back door brought everyone's head around. Rick opened the door to Nolan, freshly shaved and wearing a blue, western-styled shirt along with starched and pressed jeans.

Nolan ambled in, remembering to remove his

hat a beat later than he should have. " 'Morning, everyone. Hope I'm not interruptin' anything."

Rick fell into the role of host with incredible ease, taking the initiative of offering hospitality away from Lillian and Chandra. "You weren't interrupting a thing. Sit down and have some breakfast with us. Ty helped cook it, and did a great job."

"These are wonderful eggs, darling," Chandra said softly, smiling at her son. He was practically glowing with all the praise, and she felt a tug of guilt. Cooking eggs was such a little thing, but it had given him a lot of pleasure. Back home their meals were usually so rushed, she had never even thought about teaching him the rudiments of cooking. She'd just have to do better, she resolved.

"They sure are," Lillian seconded.

"I've had breakfast, thanks. But I thought I'd bring you some preserves." With a self-conscious movement Nolan plunked a jar of prickly-pear preserves down on the table.

"That was nice of you," Rick said. "At least have a cup of coffee while we eat breakfast."

Nolan looked everywhere but at Lillian. "Oh, well, I don't know . . ."

"We insist," Rick said, pulling out a chair for Nolan. "Don't we, Ty?"

Ty nodded vigorously, already opening the jar of preserves.

After serving Nolan coffee, Rick took a seat and looked around the table with satisfaction. "This is nice, all of us together like this."

Chandra chewed on a piece of bacon to keep

from smiling. It struck her funny that Rick and Ty were evidently the only two people at the table having a good time.

Rick took a bite of eggs, and gave Ty the thumbs-up sign. "Nolan, I was just asking Lillian if she had ever been out to your place."

Nolan almost choked on his coffee. Lillian reached for another cigarette.

Chandra wasn't sure why, but she decided to join in whatever the game was that Rick was playing. "Nolan, Rick was telling us you have a lovely place. And I understand after the lake is in, you'll have lakefront property."

Nolan nodded.

A sudden thought struck Chandra. "Lillian, you know, I'll bet our new lake will give you a lot of really interesting scenes for a whole different series of paintings. It could be a new direction for you."

Lillian raised an eyebrow, putting her own slant on what Chandra had just said. " 'Our'? Does that mean you've decided to stay here, where you belong, in the town where you were born and raised?"

Determined not to flush, Chandra lifted her chin and returned her mother's gaze. "No. It means exactly what I said. And I also think you ought to go over to Nolan's and look around. You never know where you'll find inspiration."

"Always welcome," Nolan mumbled.

"I have all the inspiration I need, thank you. I know every pore and seam on this land, and I love every square inch of it."

Chandra swept her hand out. "All these square inches are soon going to be underwater, Lillian."

Rick saw the stubborn set of Lillian's mouth and knew that any more talk on the subject, at least for now, would do no good. He decided to work on another matter. "Ty, I was thinking that you, your mother and I could go arrowhead hunting today?"

Ty's mouth dropped open. "Arrowhead hunting? What's an arrowhead?"

Rick looked at Ty, perplexed. "You mean you've never been hunting for arrowheads?"

Even Lillian looked startled.

Chandra couldn't stop the flush this time. "We live in a city."

Rick smoothed over the moment. "Of course. Well, Ty, it's not unusual for kids who live in the city not to know, but arrowheads are the tips of arrows that once belonged to Indians who lived a long time ago. You see, many years ago, even before Christopher Columbus discovered America, Indians roamed the plains of west Texas. These Indians were the ancestors of the Comanches. You've heard of the Comanches, haven't you?"

Ty nodded, his blue eyes as wide as saucers. "Did they live on Grandma's farm?"

"Perhaps. Who knows? At any rate, I'm sure there's a good chance they traveled over this farm. And if we go exploring down by the stream that runs through this basin, I'm willing to bet we'll find all kinds."

"You'd better take the opportunity, Ty, while

you've still got the chance, since, if Mr. O'Neill has his way, this land will be underwater soon."

A troubled shadow passed over Ty's face, and Lillian immediately repented. She might be a stubborn, eccentric woman, but she loved her grandson. "It will be fun for you, Ty. And when you get back, I want to see everything you find."

Ty brightened, but Chandra threw a sidelong glance at her mother. Had she heard right? Lillian was actually giving Ty her blessing to go on an outing with Rick. The only reason she could see for her mother's change of heart was that she felt sorry for Ty because he had never been on an arrowhead hunt. And she had to admit that she did too. Of course, the count of kids who had never had such an opportunity had to be in the hundreds of thousands, but not kids who grew up in and around Monte Luna. It was a natural sport, and Chandra herself had spent many a happy afternoon walking up and down the stream, her head down, concentrating on the next great find.

Rick clapped his hands together. "Great, then it's all set. I'll go home and organize us some food and be back in a couple of hours. Chandra, you'll go with us, won't you?"

She didn't want to. To go would violate the decision she had made only a couple of hours before. On the other hand, she didn't want Ty and Rick to be alone together, either. It seemed she had no choice. She nodded her assent.

And Nolan grunted his approval.

*   *   *

Chandra raised her hand, shielding her eyes, as she watched Rick and Ty make their way along the stream. They walked slowly, side by side, with Rick resting his hand on Ty's shoulder, pointing out things of interest. The sight made her so anxious, she was suddenly aware that she was gnawing on her lower lip, but she had to admit to herself that Rick was quite good with Ty, very natural. He had a way of talking to Ty so Ty could understand. And every time the two of them were together, they seemed to draw closer to each other.

With a groan Chandra fell back onto the sun-warmed quilt and closed her eyes. She had kicked her shoes off after the delicious and filling lunch Rick had supplied. The cut-off jeans she wore were her most comfortable. The blue halter top supported, but didn't restrict. Yet she still couldn't rest. Thoughts and emotions stormed and crashed inside her—memories and pain, possibilities and problems.

With the knowledge she had now about Rick, she was willing to admit that perhaps if he'd been able to remember their night together on the mesa, if he'd known that she was pregnant, then maybe . . . just maybe, things would have turned out differently. But all the *if*'s and *maybe*'s in the world wouldn't change the past. And now it was just too late. *Surely* it was too late.

He wanted to marry her; he said he loved her. But she knew that that love would turn to fury the minute he learned Ty was his son, and there would be nothing she could do to stop it. The repercussions could be terrible, affecting not just her, but Ty.

If she only knew how she truly felt. Was it possible that the desperate "crush" of her girlhood could turn into a woman's mature love? She had no idea. The problem was, she couldn't see clearly, because her feelings of the past were clouding the present.

There was movement beside her, then weight and warmth. She felt a blade of grass graze her cheek, tickling. Opening her eyes, she saw Rick.

"Hi," he said softly. "Are you mad at me?"

Sprawled beside her as he was, with the full length of his body pressed against her, the masculine impact of him hit her hard. After he had left that morning, she had taken another shower and scrubbed the scent of his soap off her body, then used Allure in hopes of wiping his possession of her from her mind and body. She had thought it worked, until now. But the nearness of him, his musky male scent, his hard, muscled length, made the memories of the hot, loving night they had spent come crashing back.

The blade of grass brushed across her lower lip. "Aren't you talking to me?"

"Am I mad at you for proposing this arrowhead hunt, you mean? The answer is yes and no. Yes, I am, because I told you that I wanted us to stop seeing each other. And . . . no, I'm not, because I'm glad Ty has had this experience. It'll be something he'll be able to tell all his friends about when we go back to Shreveport."

She lifted her head to peer downstream for her

son. He was so far away, he appeared a tiny figure in the distance. "Will he be okay?"

"Sure. I taught him exactly what to look for."

She laid her head back down and closed her eyes. "I hope he finds at least one arrowhead. He'll be so thrilled."

"He had already found two when I left him to come back here."

"Two!" She looked at him with surprise. "That's incredible."

Rick's mouth curved into a sheepish grin. "Yeah, well . . . it was also planned."

"What do you mean?"

"As you know, sometimes you can hunt all afternoon and never find an arrowhead, and I didn't want him to be disappointed, so . . ."

"You didn't!"

He nodded, his eyes twinkling. "I salted the path along the stream with my collection of arrowheads. By the time this afternoon is over, he'll have a wonderful collection of his own."

Chandra didn't know whether to laugh or be angry. She certainly didn't know what to say.

Rick grinned at her predicament. "Who knows, he may even discover an arrowhead or two that aren't a part of my collection."

She finally found her voice. "You shouldn't have, Rick. I mean, you *really* shouldn't have. You've had that collection for years."

"And now Ty will have it."

She started to sit up, but his hand on her shoulder kept her still. "Stay here beside me. I want to ask you a question."

Her breath caught in her throat at the familiar softness that had entered his voice. "Okay, what?" Casually, as if he weren't even aware of what he was doing, he rested his hand on her upper thigh, and the bare skin beneath his hand began to heat. She shifted, but he didn't move his hand. "What?" she repeated.

"It's just that I don't understand something, and it bothers me." He frowned. "It's like you were there, in my mind, before we ever started going out together, and now the feel of you, the taste of you, the scent of you, plays in the shadows of my mind constantly."

Nervously she licked her lips. "I don't know what you mean."

He slid his hand to the inside of her thigh. "When we're together, like now"—he lightly squeezed the soft flesh of her upper leg—"I know without a doubt that you're very real. But when I'm alone at night, with only my thoughts for company, you're there, in my mind, so real that I think I'm going crazy. And the really weird thing is that it's like you've been inside me for a long, long time."

Her heart tightened with a painful sort of dread. Could it possibly be that his mind had imprinted their long-ago night together and that it had been in his subconscious all this time? And that since she had returned, certain things had begun to trigger his memory? No. It was simply too improbable.

Wasn't it?

"It's an exquisite kind of haunting, Chandra,

and I accept it. What I don't understand is why you don't feel the same thing."

His hand caressed the sensitive skin between her thighs, slowly moving upward toward the hem of her shorts, causing hotly sweet sensations to run up and down her legs, distracting her from rational thought. His actions were all the more erotic because he seemed hardly aware of what he was doing, so intensely was he concentrating on what he was saying.

"Perhaps you should just accept the way things are, Rick, instead of trying to understand and change them."

Suddenly all the gentle softness left him. His hand ceased all movement, but that didn't lessen its sensual effect, because his hand was now right up against the apex of her thighs.

He shifted his body so that he was half covering her and could look her square in the face. "You're wrong, Chandra. And I'm afraid you're also in for some rough times ahead, so fasten your seat belt."

"What do you mean?"

"I'm through playing fairly. I don't know what I'll have to do to make you love me and stay with me, but be warned. I'm going to try everything I know, scrupulous or unscrupulous. I'll shower you with diamonds and emeralds, and if that doesn't work, I'll find what makes you feel the most guilty and use that. If that doesn't work, I'll make love to you until you won't have the strength to leave me."

"Rick," she murmured huskily. "Please stop. . . ."

"No way," he returned, right before his mouth, hard and rough, found hers.

Her body began to tremble as his tongue pillaged her mouth while his hand applied pressure upward, until a dull, throbbing sweetness began between her legs.

It wasn't fair, she thought, even as she moaned in response and moved against his hand. How could she be strong, how could she ever expect to escape Monte Luna in one piece, when her body betrayed her at every turn? It took only his nearness, only his touch, only his kiss . . .

Her arms went around his neck and drew him closer.

"Where do you put your perfume?" he whispered.

Her brain was misted with desire, and his question only brought confusion. "What?"

His mouth abandoned hers, leaving her suddenly bereft, but then she felt his lips behind her ears. "Do you spray your Allure here?" His tongue came out to lick at the tiny indentation behind her earlobe.

Feverishly she twisted her head toward him "No."

"No? Then where?"

His hand had worked its way beneath the edge of her cut-offs, so that it was now inside her shorts, but on the outside of her panties, rubbing the silk against her.

"Here . . ." She scraped her fingers down the side of her neck. ". . . Here."

He went immediately to the spot and inhaled. "Oh, yes!" His breathing was heavy. "There it is. The scent that drives me out of my mind night and day." His lips dropped kisses up and down her neck, on both sides, then went back to her mouth, for a slow, thorough attack on her senses.

When he tore his mouth away this time, Chandra cried out.

"Where else do you spray the perfume?" he questioned, his mouth now hard against the pulse that hammered at the base of her throat.

Weakly she raised her arm. "Here."

He lifted his head to see. "The inside of your wrists? Of course." His mouth lavished attention on one wrist, then the other, kissing, then gently sucking at, the delicate skin. Beneath his lips, need replaced blood in the veins of her wrists. "Where else?"

"Behind . . ." Hardly capable of speaking, she stopped, licked her lips, and began again. "Behind my knees."

"Roll over."

"Rick, no, I—"

"Roll over, Chandra."

Because she was at the point where she was incapable of denying him, she did as he asked. His mouth and tongue took possession of the surprisingly responsive and erogenous skin that covered the indentation behind her knees, ravenously licking and kissing first one, then the other, while both hands massaged her denim-covered buttocks.

Her fingers curled convulsively into the quilt with a helpless hunger.

"Anyplace else?" Rick questioned, his voice a mere rasp of itself.

Her limbs felt like water, but somehow she managed to right herself. "Rick . . . Ty . . . he could be coming back any minute."

"I've been watching for him. Now, answer me."

"One more place."

His eyes blazed golden. "Where?"

"The insides of my ankles."

Slowly he leaned down and licked the pounding pulse just below her ankle bones, then sucked at the skin. Chandra's hips moved of their own volition. At this moment she wanted him more than she had ever wanted anything in her life. "Why?" she asked. "Why did you do this?"

Only after he placed a lingering kiss on the instep of her foot did he move, until he was lying full length on top of her. He cradled her face between his hands. "Because I wanted to take my fill of your fragrance, I wanted to overcome my obsession with your perfume . . . and I wanted to torture you, make you want me as much as I want you."

He rolled off her and lay beside her. Long minutes passed. Then he gave a ragged laugh. "It didn't work, dammit! It didn't work! Your perfume is in my head, and I'll go to my grave smelling it."

But part of your plan worked, Chandra thought. You made me want you so much that if Ty hadn't been close by, we would have made love. She jackknifed upright and clasped her knees tightly to her chest. She needed something to hold on to! She needed some sort of *relief!*

"I see Ty," she said, raising her arm to wave to her son, who was still some distance away.

Rick sat up too. When he spoke, his tone was carefully neutral and without emotion. "It looks like he's got his hands full."

They were talking as if the previous scene between them hadn't happened, and she knew it was for the best. "Rick, I don't know about your giving Ty your collection."

"*That* particular subject is closed, Chandra." He rolled to his feet and went to meet Ty, who was now running toward them.

Eight

"You're more than welcome to move your house onto my land," Nolan told Lillian, gazing fixedly out the window as if something interesting were riveting him there. "Or just your studio, if you wanted. Or I could build you a new studio right on the lake."

Chandra realized her mouth was open, and shut it. A quick glance at her mother told her that Lillian was feeling the same amazement.

"I don't think I've ever heard you string so many words together at one time," Lillian said.

"Only a suggestion," Nolan mumbled, turning and reaching for his hat. "Gotta go. 'Bye." He bolted for the back door without ever looking at the two women.

Chandra and Lillian stared after him. Finally

Lillian spoke. "What do you think all that was about?"

Chandra remained silent, because she was beginning to understand Nolan and why he wanted Lillian to move so badly. During the years he had been working for her, he had had ample time to come to know her, to develop a fondness for her, perhaps even more. When the lake project went through, he had probably viewed it as a godsend. Because by then he would have understood that Lillian would change her lifestyle for nothing or no one—unless it was the sure knowledge that she would have fifty feet of water over her head if she didn't.

"Chandra, I asked you what you thought that was about."

Lillian was definitely not ready for what she *really* thought, Chandra decided, so she gave her a modified version. "My guess is Nolan, in his own way, is trying to make things easier for you—to move, I mean. He's a good friend."

"Humph!" Lillian lit a cigarette, inhaled deeply, then exhaled. "People just have to understand that I want to be left alone."

"Move—then they'll leave you alone."

"It's just not fair!"

"I know." Chandra's heart went out to her mother. Right now Lillian was showing as much fear and vulnerability as she knew how. Chandra had to find a way to help her. "Pam told me something the other night that I hadn't known. She said that you rarely leave this place anymore."

Lillian rolled her shoulders dismissively. "I got tired of people."

"Lillian, tell me the truth. Is Rick right? Are you afraid that you won't be able to paint anymore if you have to move away from here?"

"Stranger things have happened." She looked away, as if the matter were of no importance. "How do I know?"

Chandra wasn't fooled by her mother's nonchalant attitude. "Lillian, your talent is true and rich. It's not just going to go away because you're forced to paint new scenes."

"You don't understand," Lillian snapped irritably, putting a match flame to the tip of another cigarette.

"Yes, I do. I understand all too well how important your painting is to you, and I have a suggestion. Why don't you go visit Nolan—" Lillian started to interrupt, but Chandra held up her hand. "Listen to me. Go visit Nolan, take your sketchbook, look around, and sketch what you see."

"Why do you think that will do any good, for heaven's sake?"

"Why do you think it won't?"

Chandra waited for Lillian's objections. They never came. Instead Lillian asked a question that stopped Chandra cold.

"If I agree to move, will you and Ty come back here to stay?"

"Lillian, we're not talking about me!"

"I know full well what we're talking about, young lady, and I asked you a question."

Lillian hadn't used that particular tone of voice with her in years. It unbalanced Chandra almost as much as the question had. As Nolan had done before, she suddenly found solace in the scenery outside the window. "You have no idea how I wish I could. I miss you terribly, and it would be great for Ty to be able to see you all the time. And there's something else, too. I've come to understand fully just how much my moving away affected you. I wish there were some way I could wave a magic wand and fix it for all of us. But . . . at least for now, it would be very hard for me to move back here."

"It's Richard O'Neill, isn't it?"

Chandra jerked around. "I beg your pardon?"

"There's something going on between you and Rick, and don't bother trying to tell me I'm wrong. Whatever it is has had you acting most peculiar about him ever since you've been home."

"No, not really—"

"Mom, Mom!" Ty came tearing into the kitchen, his face lit up with excitement. "Rick is playing baseball this afternoon, and he wants us to come watch him!"

Only a day had passed since the picnic and arrowhead hunt, and Chandra had to hand it to Rick. He was certainly fulfilling his pledge. He wasn't playing fair at all. "I don't think so, honey."

"Please, Mom, *please*. I want to go. Rick plays first base. He says he's not very good, but I bet he is, and I want to see him play."

Before she could answer Ty, Rick strode into

the kitchen, exuding that particular sensual magnetism that had haunted her through the years and continued to be so disturbing to her now. "Good morning, Chandra, Lillian. Great day, isn't it?"

"Don't you ever work?" she asked crossly, sorry an instant later, because her remark caused both Ty and Lillian to cast her an odd look.

"Not on Saturday." He sprawled, uninvited and unperturbed, in a chair across from her and gave her a grin. "So has Ty told you about the game? It's O'Neill employees against O'Neill management, and it's always a lot of fun."

"We've got things to do."

"What?" Ty asked.

"Things," she answered lamely, determined to come up with something Ty would really love.

"Come on, Chandra," Rick murmured softly. "How dangerous can a softball game be? You'll be sitting up in the stands in the middle of a crowd, and I'll be out on the field. Besides, you can watch me get beat."

"I seem to remember your lettering in baseball every year you went out for it."

"That was a long time ago."

"A lot of things were," she snapped, before she could stop herself. Rick's invitation to the baseball game had managed to aggravate the tension that had been building in her during the hours of the sleepless night she had just spent.

"Mom! I've never seen a real baseball game before."

Her overactive nerves made her sharp with Ty. "That's nonsense, Ty! You play Little League at home."

"Aw, Little League is not the same thing at all."

This was all Rick's fault, Chandra thought, nearly gnashing her teeth.

Unexpectedly Lillian spoke up. "I'm not aware of anything you had planned this afternoon."

"I'm sure that anything that was planned can be changed," Rick said smoothly. "Isn't that right, Chandra?"

"If you say so," she muttered.

He smiled. "Why don't you and Ty come in your car, and I'll see you there."

A glance at her son's hopeful face gave her her answer. "Fine."

Rick and his team were already out on the field, warming up, when she and Ty arrived. He had evidently been watching for her, because the minute he saw them, he trotted over.

As she watched him approach, she was aware of a warmth creeping into her limbs. Wearing shorts and a team jersey, Rick, to her mind, looked quite simply magnificent.

He stopped in front of her. "Hi. Glad you could make it," he murmured. Then, as if it were the most natural thing in the world, he bent to kiss her.

She gasped in surprise. "Rick! Not in front of all these people!" She looked up at him and was snared by the astonishingly intimate gleam in his eyes.

"Then later?" he asked.

Her throat went dry. Damn! How could he make her blood heat in front of all these people?

Ty pulled on his jersey. "Rick, Rick, when does the game start?"

Affectionately he ruffled Ty's hair. "In just a few minutes. You and your mom better go on up and grab yourselves seats."

"Good idea. Come on, Ty."

Rick grabbed her wrist. "Later?"

She temporized with, "We'll see," not wanting to start an argument in front of so many interested spectators.

Chandra and Ty made their way up the steps of the rapidly filling stands. Shirley, the head buyer for O'Neill's, waved a friendly hello, as did quite a few other people. Although she had come to the game against her better judgment, Chandra began to relax. The late-afternoon sun was warm on her bare arms, and she was glad she had worn the cool ivory cotton camisole with lace trim and the full skirt of browns and golds that ended mid-calf in a flounced hem. Leather sandals completed her comfortable outfit.

She smiled at first one person, then another, feeling completely at home. She had grown up with most of these people, and as a young girl she had sat in these stands many times.

A shout of "Chandra! Over here!" reached her ears, and she glanced around to see Pam waving frantically at her. "Over here! We've saved you a place."

"I didn't know you all were going to be here,"

Chandra said once she and Ty were settled beside Pam and Robert.

Since Pam was sitting between Robert and Chandra, he leaned forward so that he could speak to her. "I wouldn't miss one of Rick's games, and this one"—he jerked his thumb at his wife—"wouldn't be left at home."

Chandra frowned worriedly at her friend. "Aren't you uncomfortable?"

"Sure," Pam said cheerfully, "but I'd be just as uncomfortable at home. Why not be uncomfortable where I can have a little fun?"

Robert rolled his eyes at his wife's logic. Chandra shook her head.

The sound of "Play ball!" came over the loudspeaker, and all attention turned to the field. The crowd's enthusiasm rose, rivaling that at a major league game.

Chandra tried to match the exuberance of the people around her, to get caught up in the game, but she soon realized it was no use. Her entire concentration was focused on Rick. As far as she was concerned, there was no one else on the field.

It was an unbidden reaction, and one that took her totally by surprise, but for once she didn't try to stifle her responses. Perhaps the crowd around her and the distance that lay between her and Rick played a part in Chandra's allowing herself not to censor her feelings. There was no doubt that she felt a certain sense of safety, of anonymity. But whatever the reason, for the first time since she had started seeing Rick, she let her emotions flow unchecked.

Without feeling that she shouldn't, she observed the strength of his legs as he bent to scoop up a ball, the power of his arms as he threw, the agility of his body as he stretched to reach a wild pitch.

She followed every move he made, a hunger in her eyes, a fire in her blood.

Then Rick turned and looked straight at her. He saw the hunger and the fire that she was unknowingly radiating, and he in turn responded. The noise receded, the crowd became invisible, the action faded away. For him there was only Chandra, with her glorious flaxen hair rippling around her face, and her fragrance, mysterious and enticing, seemingly blowing to him on the breeze.

Too late, he saw the ball coming straight at him.

Up in the stands Chandra watched, horrified. She heard the crack of the bat as it connected with the ball. She watched, as if in slow motion, the ball fly straight at Rick. With killing velocity, it struck his head, and he went down as she screamed.

Before Pam or Robert could restrain her, she was up and running as fast as she could, down the steps of the bleachers and out onto the field. Players were already kneeling around Rick when she got to him, but she pushed them aside. Then what she saw made her gasp in fear. Blood poured from a gash on his temple. His eyes were closed, and her first thought was that he was unconscious. Everything she had ever read about the seriousness of head injuries came rushing back to her.

She dropped to the ground beside him. "Rick! Oh, my God, Rick!" Her hand shook as she wiped the dirt off his face. "Rick, say something! Talk to me!"

Slowly his eyes opened. "What do you want me to say?"

Unaware of the tears running down her face, she sobbed in relief.

Someone attempted to lift her by her arms. "Let the doctor see to him now."

Rick stirred, raising his arm to pull her back down to him. "Let her alone!"

She stroked her hand across his forehead, attempting to soothe him. "Don't worry. I'm not going anywhere."

His lips lifted into a smile.

"Well, well, what's all the hysteria about? Let's have a look-see." Dr. Murphy, who had been in charge of the medical side of the high-school athletic program for as long as Chandra could remember, pushed his way to Rick and knelt down on the other side of him. The now silver-haired doctor directed a stern look down at Rick. "In all my years of watching you play, Richard O'Neill, I don't think I've ever seen you do such a stupid thing. What happened? It looked like you were daydreaming, but that couldn't be, because you *know* better than that."

Rick rubbed his head and grinned ruefully. "I'm afraid that's exactly what I was doing."

The doctor put on his glasses and peered at the wound. "The bleeding looks like it's about stopped. Good thing for you, you saw the ball at the last minute, or this could have been a lot worse."

Rick struggled to sit up, and Chandra helped him. "I lost my balance while I was trying to get out of the way. I think the ball just grazed my temple."

The doctor grunted his agreement and applied a temporary dressing. "Stunned you. Is there someone who can drive you home?"

Chandra spoke up quickly. "I can."

"Good. Just clean the wound up with a little hydrogen peroxide and water." He turned back to Rick. "I don't think there's anything serious, but you know the routine. Your head may ache a little, but if the pain gets bad or you have trouble with your vision or with nausea, you get yourself to the hospital pronto and have them call me." Dr. Murphy got to his feet, and several hands came out to help Chandra and Rick up.

Chandra held on to Rick's arm, as much to steady herself as to steady him. She was hoping no one would notice how upset she was, but she should have known better.

The doctor looked at her over the rim of his glasses and directed his parting words to her. "Don't look so worried, young woman. Rick was always a tough kid."

That brought a round of laughter from Rick's fellow weekend athletes, and those in the stands burst into applause at the sight of him up and walking off the field.

Robert was waiting for them at the side of the field. "Don't worry about Ty, Chandra. Pam and I will run him out to Lillian's after the game."

"Thanks." That was one worry off her mind, at

least, Chandra thought as she led Rick to her car. But she had another one. A *big* one. As she had watched that ball speed toward an unsuspecting Rick, an indisputable fact had come bursting to light within her. *She loved Rick.* She loved him with all her heart.

On the drive up to the mesa, Chandra kept a worried watch on Rick. He was uncharacteristically quiet, lying back against the seat with his eyes closed.

Once there, she tried to assist him into the house, but he put his arm around her and walked in on his own power. She found the first aid kit with no problem. The problem came in getting Rick to take his injury seriously.

"Will you sit down and let me do this?" she asked, more than a little put out. As scared as she had been for him, the least he could do was cooperate with her efforts to help him.

"It's nothing, I tell you," he said, fishing in the refrigerator for a beer.

She took the beer out of his hand. "Fruit juice, water, maybe ice tea. No beer."

His eyes sparkled mischievously. "I'll let you play nurse if you'll let me have a beer."

She put her hands on her hips. "You'll let me clean your head up, and you won't have any beer!"

He sighed and shook his head. "You're a hard woman."

She had to do something constructive, she decided, or any minute, reaction would set in and she would burst into tears. Her emotions had never felt more fragile than at this moment. "That's right. Now, sit." She made a solution of hydrogen peroxide and water in a bowl and reached for the cotton. "Ty gives me less trouble than you do," she muttered. "Will you keep still!"

For the first time Rick's face took on a serious expression. "I hope Ty wasn't too upset by my getting hit."

Her hand flew to her head in consternation, and she groaned. "Oh, no!"

"What's wrong?"

"I ran out of the stands without giving him a moment's thought. I can't believe it!"

He took her hand in his and squeezed it. "Chandra, don't do that to yourself. I sometimes think you're way too hard on yourself as a mother."

She couldn't resist the jab. "A fact that you haven't hesitated to take advantage of lately." She jerked her hand away. "Do I need to bring up the arrowhead hunt and the game this afternoon?"

"You know my reasons, and I won't apologize, especially if it produces the desired results. The point in this case is, you knew Ty was safe with friends, but you weren't sure about me."

He was too close to the truth for comfort. She dabbed at his wound extra hard.

"Ow!"

"Don't be a baby," she mumbled. Still her ministrations turned more gentle, and soon she was finished. "There. The doctor was right. It's not too bad." She straightened and looked at him critically. "How are you feeling? Does your head ache?"

"Not much."

"Are you hungry?"

He gazed at her thoughtfully. "For what?"

She knew that look. "For food," she returned firmly.

"Ah. Well, as a matter of fact, I am. I'll bet you are too." He got up. "Since we're going to miss out on the barbeque, why don't I check on what I've got in the freezer?"

She pushed him back into the chair. "Oh, no, you don't! I'll do that. You sit still and rest."

"Chandra, I'm not an invalid."

"Maybe not, but a small portion of caution won't hurt a thing." Poking her head in the refrigerator, she found it well stocked with basics—nothing fancy, but enough so that she could whip up a couple of ham-and-cheese omelets, along with a salad. She began assembling the ingredients.

"I was sort of looking forward to a steak."

He sounded so wistful, she had to smile. "I read somewhere that you should eat lightly after an injury."

Instead of the teasing remark she expected, his come-back was serious. "I don't think I've ever been so well taken care of. Thank you."

"It's nothing."

Chandra barely noticed when Rick lapsed into silence during their meal, since her own thoughts were weighing so heavily on her mind. Up until the point when she had thought he was in danger, she had refused even to concede the possibility that she could love him. While acknowledging her physical need of him, she had only been able to see the negative side of any commitment with him that might extend past the next evening. Now she realized she had been giving the past too much importance, that the past had been with her for far too long.

She also realized she desperately needed to be alone to sort things out. The revelation that she loved Rick was going to force her to rearrange her entire thinking, maybe her entire life.

"You're barely eating," Rick pointed out.

She glanced up, forcing a bright smile. "I guess I wasn't as hungry as I thought."

"Too bad. The omelet's wonderful."

"Thank you." She gathered up her plate and glass and took them to the sink. "You know," she said over her shoulder, "you're doing fine now. I think I could probably leave. You don't need me anymore."

"You're wrong," he murmured in that soft voice that undid her every time she heard it. "I need you very much."

She kept her back to him, rinsing off her plate. "I should get home and see about Ty."

"He's fine and you know it."

"Still—"

"Come here, Chandra." Slowly she turned around. "Come here," he repeated.

"I don't think that would be a very good idea."

"And I don't think it would be a very good idea if you left me. What if I get a severe headache? What if I get double vision?"

She knew she was being blackmailed. "Call the doctor."

"What if I'm in so much pain that I can't make it to the phone?"

"Rick, stop it! I know what you're doing!"

"What? What am I doing, Chandra?"

"You told me that you were going to try everything you knew, scrupulous or unscrupulous, and now you're doing just that, trying to play on my emotions."

"If you're so sure that's what I'm doing," he said softly, "then leave."

Damn him! Rick knew good and well that if she thought there was the slightest danger that he might take ill in the next few hours, she'd stay.

He saw the resigned look in her eyes and smiled. "Good. Now come here. Please."

She made her way across the kitchen to his side. "What is it?"

He leaned his head against the high back of the kitchen chair and gazed up at her. "Just one kiss, Chandra. I want just one kiss. I really need it."

Her entire body began to ache with the very same need. "Just one?"

He nodded, drawing her down to him until she was sitting on his lap. "This is much better," he murmured huskily, his mouth close to her lips.

"You're horrible," she whispered.

"Horrible," he agreed. "Did you know that right before I saw that ball heading for me, I thought I could smell your perfume?"

With his hard, bare thighs beneath her, she could feel her resistance melting away. "That's ridiculous."

Now his lips were so close that when he spoke, they grazed hers. "I know. Ridiculous."

"Rick . . . just one kiss . . . right?"

"Right," he murmured, and his tongue dipped into her mouth.

His kiss was so gentle, it never occurred to her to hold back in any way. Not when it felt so good to open her mouth, let her tongue touch and rub against his, then plunge deep into his mouth. Cradled in his arms, she clung to him and gave herself up to the feeling of utter ecstasy that only his kisses could bring her.

Rick had meant to ask her about the tears he had seen on her face when he'd opened his eyes and found her beside him after the ball had hit him. She had been desperately worried about him, that much was obvious, and he couldn't help wondering, *hoping*, that her worry meant she loved him. But with her on his lap, her soft buttocks nestling so sweetly over his manhood, he could feel himself growing hard. Priorities quickly became rearranged in his mind as he decided there would be time enough later to question her. For now, it was urgent that this throbbing, aching pain he felt should be assuaged within her.

Slowly, he unbuttoned her camisole, parting the material, and exposing her breasts to his hungry gaze. "Lord, Chandra, you are so beautiful, so full." He slid his hand over the soft, soft skin, caressing and cupping her.

"And your nipples"—his fingers closed on one taut bud—"so hard, so tight! I've got to have a taste, just one. May I?"

Chandra realized that Rick was actually asking her permission. She had heard the trembling in his voice as he asked, and knew he wanted badly to taste her. Perhaps almost as badly as she wanted him to taste her. "Oh, yes, oh, yes! Now, please!"

As his mouth found the tip, it was like a match set to gasoline. The hot pleasure burst into flames, shooting directly to her loins and burning there, waiting to be put out. Arching against him, she whispered, "Don't stop."

He complied. Restlessly, her own hands wove through his hair, then played over his chest, until finally she tugged his baseball jersey up. Her goal was to feel her breasts pressed against the soft reddish-brown hair of his chest.

He helped, pulling his shirt over his head and throwing it across the kitchen. Moments later her camisole joined it. And then they were straining against each other, reveling in the fire that the friction of their two bodies was causing.

They kissed, but he couldn't seem to stay away from her breasts, and soon the suckling at her breast resumed. The feeling was exquisitely unbearable to Chandra. She had never known anything like it.

Until . . . he shifted her on his lap in such a way that her legs were slightly spread. Her skirt had already worked itself to above her knees, and his hand glided down her hip. For a moment he caressed the pulsing skin behind her knee, then slowly began to travel upward, under her skirt.

Chandra quivered in anticipation, knowing that the magic of Rick's touch could take her to the very threshold of ecstasy and, if he so chose, beyond.

But he stopped.

"I've got to have just one touch, Chandra. Just one."

She heard the raggedness of his breathing, and, dazed by passion as she was, it almost seemed to her that he was begging. Desire clogged her throat so, no words would come. She nodded, and hoped he understood.

He must have, because his hand stroked beneath her skirt to the edge of her panties, then under, to the very core of her desire. Devastated, she squirmed against him, feeling his throbbing hardness against her hips.

He groaned as if he were in agony. "Chandra, Chandra, you're so moist. I want you. Tell me you want me. Let me make love to you. Let me."

Shuddering, she held him close. Her tongue licked into the shell of his ear and her breath was warm and quick. "Yes, yes, yes, yes, yes, yes, yes, yes . . ."

Holding her tightly, Rick slid with her to the kitchen floor. All remaining clothes came off. Then he drove into her, and continued until their mutual, bone-searing passion had been completely vanquished. At least temporarily.

Nine

Sometime in the early morning hours they parted, with Rick making Chandra promise she would see him that night. They had things they needed to discuss, he said, and Chandra didn't hesitate to agree.

She spent the day searching her heart and her mind. Certain things were no longer in doubt. She loved Rick, and she wanted a future with him. But before the two of them could have a future together, there would have to be honesty between them.

She had to tell him that Ty was his son. The fallout might equal that from an atomic bomb, but there was no question that she had to tell him. Her love for him had convinced her he had a right to know.

For the time being, she decided, she would hold

off telling Ty. Whether she would eventually tell him would depend on how Rick took the news. There was every possibility that Rick might categorically refuse to believe her. After all, he had no memory of that night. And if he thought she was lying and he wanted no part of Ty as his son, then Ty need never be involved. They would go back to Shreveport and resume their life, and she would be wiser and very much sadder.

But there was one person she needed to tell first, the one person who had suffered the most from her pregnancy besides herself—Lillian.

That evening Chandra began getting ready early for her date with Rick, donning the second of the two dresses she had bought at O'Neill's. It was the type so popular now, a strapless dress in aqua polished cotton. The bodice was lightly boned and the skirt was a full circle. As she did every time she went out, she dabbed Allure on all her pulse points. Lastly, she looked at her hair. As usual, the flaxen length haloed her head and face in a wildly waving mass. She shook her head in despair at the sight, and went to find Lillian.

In her studio Lillian spared a brief glance at Chandra before returning her attention to the canvas in front of her. "Going out again?"

"Yes." Chandra perched on a stool, her mind busy sorting through what would be the best way to tell Lillian. The feeling of being seventeen years old again came back to her—the awkwardness of her situation, the confusion over doing the right thing, even the fear of hurting her mother. This was going to be very hard for her. Lillian had never given her anything but support and love, and the last thing Chandra would ever want to do would be to cause her more pain. *Where did she start?*

"When Robert brought Ty home after the game, he told me that Richard had been hit by a ball," Lillian remarked conversationally. "I gather you were taking care of him last night."

Chandra listened closely to the tone of Lillian's words, but she could find no criticism there. "Uh, yes. He's fine, though."

"Good, that's good." She set down her brush and stood back, studying her canvas. "By the way, while you and Ty were at the game, I took a ride."

"Oh?" Chandra was beginning to get the feeling that Lillian had something on her mind other than her painting.

"I drove out toward Nolan's place. Didn't stop in to visit, you understand, just kind of looked around. Hadn't been over that way in years."

"What'd you think?"

"Richard was right. It's quite nice around there. Now, if I could find myself something equally nice and interesting, I might buy it."

"Land that would prove interesting to paint, you mean?"

Lillian nodded brusquely, turning to face her daughter and reaching for her ever-present cigarettes at the same time. "Chandra . . . have you given any more thought to moving back here?"

Here was her chance, she thought. Here was an opening. She only needed the courage. "Yes," she said slowly, "I have. Lillian . . . there's something I need to talk with you about."

Lillian puffed out a cloud of smoke. "Does it have anything to do with Richard O'Neill?"

"Yes."

Lillian nodded. "It's gotten serious between you, hasn't it?" She sighed heavily. "I've seen it coming, and if you want to know the truth, it's part of the reason I'm considering moving."

"I don't understand."

Shrugging, Lillian grinned. "I would think it was obvious. I couldn't very well go on opposing my son-in-law, now, could I? And much as I hate the idea of having to leave my home, if marrying him will keep you and Ty here, it would be worth it to me to give in and move."

"You don't understand. Just listen, please." Chandra slid off the stool and began pacing around the studio. "It's true that what I need to talk with you about has to do with Rick and me, but . . . what I want to tell you about all began years ago, when I was a teenager." She glanced at her mother and saw her cigarette suspended midway to her lips. "Rick is Ty's father."

Lillian slumped back against a counter, the cigarette in her hand forgotten. "I should have known. I should have known."

"There was no way for you or anyone to know. It was just one night. There was no other connection between Rick and me, and Ty certainly doesn't resemble Rick."

Carefully, methodically, Lillian snubbed out her cigarette. "I never really wanted to know who Ty's father was, because I was afraid of what I would do. I lost you, and that just about killed me."

Chandra went to her mother and put her arms around her, hugging her. "I know, and I'm so sorry."

"He's the reason you've refused to come back all these years, isn't he?"

Chandra pulled away, nodding.

"I should have known. I'm an artist. I've seen Rick and Ty together. I should have noticed the lines, the bone structure . . . *something!*"

"It wouldn't have changed anything."

"It might have. For instance, I might have pulled the trigger on that shotgun I held on him."

That drew a small smile from Chandra. "I'm glad you didn't, because, Mom . . . I love him."

Lillian gazed at her for a long moment, her eyes moist with emotion. "You called me Mom," she said softly. Then louder, in a voice closer to her own, she asked, "Does Rick know?"

"No. But I'm going to tell him tonight."

Lillian held out her arms, and once again Chandra went into them. "I love you. Whatever happens, I love you and Ty. I don't want either of you to be hurt."

Chandra brushed away a tear. "I'll be okay, and don't worry, I won't let Ty get hurt."

Rick's big, powerful car hummed along the highway, cutting through the night with ease.

"Are we going to your house?" Chandra asked.

He glanced over at her and smiled. "Close by. I

know a spot out on Sky Mesa that I thought would be a good place for us to talk. Besides, it's too great a night to stay indoors. Okay?"

She nodded. "Sure."

Chandra stared out the side window, thinking. In some strange way it was fitting and right that they park out on the mesa tonight. The mesa was where their story had begun, and coincidentally, tonight was very much like that night nine years before. The stars had been out in full force then too. The wind had been cool and gentle, just as it was now. It was even the same time of year—the end of school, the time of her senior prom. And off in the distance a storm was brewing, completing for Chandra the perfect sense of déjà vu.

Maybe the mesa would be where their story would end, too. But how would it end? Angrily, hurtfully, or happily?

Rick left the road, and the big car bumped over uneven ground, driving farther and farther away from the road and houses, until finally Rick pulled to a stop. Chandra opened her door and got out. To the northwest, lightning bolts slashed the black velvet sky. But here, at the spot Rick had chosen, the stars still glimmered and the wind was caressing. Only an occasional cloud moving over the moon told her that the storm might be heading in their direction.

As Rick retrieved a large quilt from the trunk, he, too, glanced up at the sky. "I don't think we have anything to worry about. The storm may not even get this far, and at any rate, if it does, it'll take awhile." He spread the quilt over the ground.

Sitting down on it, he held out his hand. "Join me?"

Rick watched her as she came down beside him, marveling at the way the moon and stars highlighted her pale beauty. Her scent came to him, bedeviling him on some basic level, taunting him with that unique and powerful mixture of white flowers, a heavy portion of sensuality, a dash of the moon's mystique, and a splattering of a star-filled heaven.

Her hair shimmered with a life of its own, witchy and untamed. Her breasts rose high and firm beneath a strapless aqua dress, making him long to take it off her.

If it were true that the eye was the camera of the mind, then he would have this picture of her with him always. Suddenly, out of some dim recess of his mind, a glimmer of a similar picture flashed, then vanished. He frowned.

Chandra had been observing the changing expressions that chased across his face, and she saw the frown. "What's wrong?"

For perhaps a second or two he studied her, an odd look on his face. But then he smiled. "Nothing. I was just trying to decide how I was going to keep my hands off you while we talked." With a gesture he couldn't control, he reached to run his fingers across her collarbone, then chuckled at himself. "I guess that answers my question. I can't."

Her skin heated at his touch, and before she could subdue it, desire flamed in her eyes.

He saw the desire and shook his head. "Don't

do that! I have to keep my hands off you, at least for a while, because I want us to talk."

Her throat was dry from nerves. She cleared it. "You're right. We need to."

"Good." He stretched his long length out on the quilt. "Look at the stars, Chandra. They seem close enough to touch."

She lay down beside him and, as he was doing, looked up at the sky. Dazzled by the beauty, she held up her arm to test his theory. "I can almost touch them."

He chuckled. "Some people say that our fates are written in the stars."

"If that were the case," she said quietly, "and we could learn to read the stars, it sure would save a lot of wear and tear on us, wouldn't it? I mean, we wouldn't have to agonize over each and every decision, trying to make sure we were doing the right thing. We could just come out here, look up at the stars, and know exactly what to do."

Rick heard the wistfulness in her voice, and rose on one elbow so that he could gaze down into her face. "I don't have to read the stars, Chandra, to know that you and I were meant to be together."

"You think it's that simple?"

"Absolutely. I've seen this sky every night of my life, but it takes on a new beauty when I see it with you. And the strange thing is, that holds true for every aspect of my life."

She knew what he meant. When a person was in love, every experience seemed heightened, intensified. But she wasn't quite ready to say it yet. What happened here tonight would decide the rest of her life, and in her chest there was a tight, painful pressure in acknowledgment of that fact.

He brushed a finger across her cheek, then took up a flaxen curl and began to rub it between his thumb and forefinger. "Chandra . . . it really scared you when I went down at the baseball game yesterday, didn't it?"

She kept her eyes trained on the stars. Somehow it was easier than looking at him. "Yes."

She said it softly, but he heard, and it gave him hope. "When I opened my eyes and saw you . . . there were tears on your face."

"Head injuries can be tricky. I was concerned."

"Is that all there was to it?"

"No. There was something else."

Her quiet, slow words had Rick holding his breath, waiting for what she would say next. He practically had to bite his tongue to keep from prompting her, but it was vitally important to him that each word she spoke be her own and come from her heart.

She turned her head to face him. "I had been fighting the truth for days, but when I saw the ball heading straight toward your head, there was no doubt . . . I knew at that moment that I loved you."

"Chandra!"

"No, listen. There's something else—"

"You'll never know how I've wanted to hear those words from you!" Having Chandra say she loved him had hit Rick like a potent narcotic rush. Every corpuscle in his body was threatening to burst with happiness. "Say it again."

"I love you . . . but, Rick—"

His mouth came down and blotted out her next words. Caught up in a natural high, he was incapable of listening or talking. A hot urgency was rushing through his veins, and it was *that* call he heeded. Rick shifted his body until he was lying full length over her.

Somewhere, distant thunder rumbled, but Rick didn't hear it. Running around and around in his brain was the knowledge that Chandra loved him. He had finally succeeded in making her forget the man who had hurt her. *Chandra loved him!* That fact pushed everything else out of his mind. That and the incredible feel of her beneath him.

Supporting his weight on his elbows, he combed his fingers through her flaxen hair, which, even in the dim light, seemed to shine. There was something gloriously barbaric about Chandra's hair, he decided.

Her breasts mounded above the strapless neckline, creamy and tempting, but the aqua dress hid from his view the pink nipples. He brushed his thumb across one and, through the material, felt it spring to life. He wanted her nipple in his mouth; he wanted her breast in his hand.

Wait, his mind told him. *Wait.* But his body had no patience, and his lips hungrily sought her throat, savoring the softness of her skin and the erotic scent of her perfume.

He raised her skirt and ground his pelvis against hers, enjoying the exquisite pleasure and pain of being so close to the moment when he would have her. Soon she would be completely undressed, her long legs around his back, and she would be writhing against him. With an intimate undulation of his hips he applied pressure to that sensitive spot between her thighs, and heard her moan.

Rick wasn't sure how much longer he could wait, but he wanted to prolong this lovemaking as much as he could. For tonight was a night he would remember all his life, a night like no other. A night when all the elements of nature were at their best—dazzling lightning, beguiling stars, cooling wind. A night when Chandra, soft, sweet, and pliant with passion, was lying beneath him, with her hair radiantly encircling her head like a band of light, her aqua strapless dress pushed up around her waist, and her perfume whirling around in his brain like some haunting melody that never would leave.

Rick went still. His blood froze. A pulse in his temple pounded.

Chandra opened her eyes, confused. "Rick?"

Suddenly his memory was crystal-clear. *This had all happened before!*

"Rick?"

"*I* hurt you," he whispered hoarsely, staring down at her with eyes that were filled with horrified realization. "Oh, God, Chandra, it was *me* who hurt you!" He rolled off her onto his back and flung his forearm across his eyes.

Chandra sat up and hugged her knees to her chest. Cold fear washed over her as she waited for his reaction.

"It was here, on the mesa, wasn't it?" he asked quietly.

She nodded.

"When?" She hesitated, and Rick jackknifed into a sitting position. "When, Chandra?"

"The night of my senior prom, nine years ago."

He closed his eyes for a moment, as if even the light from the stars and the distant lightning were too harsh. "That's right, I remember. It was the night before my dad died, and I was drunk." A thin, mirthless thread of laughter escaped him. "It was the last time I ever got drunk. God!" Unable to sit still, he stood up and shoved his hands into his pockets.

Thunder sounded, closer now. Even the wind had picked up. Chandra hugged her knees more tightly. "What made you remember?"

"I don't know. A combination of things, I suppose. Our minds must imprint images and scents without our assistance or our knowledge." He rubbed his hand around the back of his neck. "That perfume of yours has been driving me crazy ever since I smelled it that day at Robert's. It's incredible, but on some level I remembered Chandra's Allure, and it teased me night and day."

He knelt and took hold of a handful of her hair. "And then there was your hair. How could I have forgotten it? It was what made me cross the room that night and ask you to dance." His voice softened. "I used you that night, didn't I? I'm so sorry, baby."

Tears clouded Chandra's vision, and she brushed at them so that she could see him clearly. "You didn't know what you were doing."

"Don't make excuses for me!" He jerked to his

feet. "Dear Lord, when I think of what I did! No wonder you didn't want to have anything to do with me when you came back. You must have thought I was a first-class bastard."

"I did, I admit it. But, Rick, that was before I got to know you, *really* know you."

With his hands on his hips he gazed bleakly down at her. "You realize that if we hadn't come out here tonight I might never have remembered? Scent is supposed to be the strongest memory trigger there is, but tonight there was also the place, and the circumstances, and . . . Hell! You were even wearing an aqua dress that night, weren't you?"

"Yes," she said, miserable. "I had already planned to tell you tonight, Rick. You're angry with yourself, but I'm not blameless in this."

"You! You were just a young girl." He came down beside her again, only this time he sat. Stroking her hair back from her face he murmured, "Nine years ago you were completely innocent, a virgin." He shook his head in disgust. "Nine years ago."

"Rick, don't be so hard on yourself," she begged.

But he wasn't listening. Suddenly he had stiffened. When he turned toward her she saw the most agonizing torment she had ever seen in the expression on a human face. His mouth moved, but no words came.

A raw pain seared through Rick's chest. He clamped his hand around Chandra's forearm, so powerfully that he was sure he was hurting her, but he couldn't seem to relax his hold. His muscles felt as if they had tightened to the point of rigidity. Slowly, his voice cracking with emotion, he whispered, "Ty is my son, isn't he?"

Tears streamed freely down her face, and she nodded.

"Oh, my God. Oh, my God." He dropped his face into his hands and began to cry.

Unbearably affected by his suffering, she rose on her knees and put her arms around him, trying to absorb the tremors of his body. "Don't, Rick. Stop it. You didn't remember, and knowing you as I do now, I wish I'd tried harder to tell you, but then—"

Raising his hand, he swiped impatiently at the moisture that covered his face. "You tried to tell me?"

She released him and briefly looked away, unwillingly recalling the hell of that day in his office. "Yes. I came to your office one day, but"—she shrugged—"I don't know. You walked right past me."

Anguished eyes stared at her. Tentatively his hand came out to touch her face. "Can you ever forgive me?"

"Of course! I meant what I said earlier. I love you, Richard O'Neill! And I couldn't have told you that if I were still harboring any bitterness or hate. Coming home, getting to know you, and falling in love with you have taught me a lot." She managed a tremulous laugh. "I was afraid you'd hate me when I told you that Ty was your son."

"Hate you?" He gathered her into his arms and cradled her close against him. "Chandra, when I think of what you went through by yourself, I could die. You were so young, and you must have been scared out of your mind. I'll never, ever be able to make it up to you."

"There's no reason for you to try." She pushed away from him so that she could see his face. It was important that he understand how she felt. "You were just a few years older than I was. Who can say? Even if you'd known I was pregnant and had done the right thing by marrying me, it might not have worked out. Looking back, I can see how extremely immature both of us were. But, Rick, now we've found something precious that I don't want us to lose."

"I love you," he said, hearing his voice shake and not caring.

Lightning flashed directly over their heads, illuminating Rick's tear-stained face. "I was so afraid you'd hate me," she whispered, "or that you wouldn't believe me when I told you."

"I'll tell you something. If I hadn't remembered on my own and you had told me, I would have accepted what you said without question. Do you know why?"

"No."

Spanning her jaw with his hand, he raised her face to his. "Because I would have wanted it to be true so badly."

She nearly cried then. "I love you."

Rick bent and placed a tender kiss on her lips. "Does Ty know?"

"No. As he's gotten older, he's asked about his father, of course, but I've told him only that I had a relationship when I was very young that didn't work out. I never touched on the pain involved. Instead I've stressed to him over and over again how very lucky I consider myself, because that brief relationship gave him to me."

Sadly, Rick shook his head. "You've been through so much, raising him alone. We'll tell him, but not until you think the time is right. In the meantime I'm looking forward to getting closer to my son." A look of amazement crossed his face. *"My son,"* he repeated softly.

Thunder boomed, causing Rick to lift his eyes to search the sky. "The storm's nearly here. Let's go back to Lillian's." His voice thickened with emotion. "I want to see my son."

Ten

The night turned violent and angry, with the storm breaking before they got home. Rain poured down in hard, driving sheets. In spite of the fact that Chandra was inside Rick's car, dry and protected from the storm's wrath, she unexpectedly shivered. A chill was permeating her skin, and anxiety was twisting her insides into knots.

Rick steered his car to a stop in front of Lillian's house and switched off the engine. "I can hardly wait to see Ty."

"He'll be asleep," Chandra warned.

"That's okay. It'll be a new experience, watching my son sleep." Suddenly he reached to switch on the overhead light and studied her for a moment. "What's wrong, Chandra? I can practically feel your nervous tension over here."

"I'm not sure. I guess I'm scared. I haven't been

really happy for such a long time, and now it almost seems too easy. Do you really think we've got a chance?"

Very gently, he took her face between his hands. "We've got more than a chance. I love you, you love me, and we both love Ty. There's no doubt about it. The three of us are going to be very, very happy."

"I guess it's just hard for me to believe that things could turn out right after being wrong for so long," she said, then caught a movement out of the corner of her eye. Chandra peered through the thin film of condensation that had formed on the window. "That's funny. Lillian is standing on the front porch like she's waiting for us."

"She must have heard us drive up." Rick leaned forward to wipe clear a portion of the window. "She doesn't have the shotgun. I think that's a good sign, don't you?" He reached into the back seat and pulled up an umbrella.

Chandra laughed, thinking how good Rick was for her. Instead of concentrating on the knots of unease in her stomach, she should be counting her lucky stars. She threw her arms around him and kissed him. "I think it's definitely a good sign."

Shaking his head, he said, "Do that again, lady, and Lillian will have cause to come marching out here with her shotgun, because I will be ravaging her daughter."

"Ravaging! Really?"

Throwing her a playful warning look, Rick opened the door and hoisted the umbrella. "Come on, let's go."

Giggling like children, they ran across the yard and up the steps to the porch. "Lillian, what are you doing out here? It's pouring!" Rick exclaimed, then went still at the expression on Lillian's face.

Brushing the rain off her skirt and arms, Chandra glanced up and caught her first sight of her mother. By the light of the porch lamp Lillian looked haggard, her face completely colorless. "My Lord, what's wrong?"

"It's Ty. I think he's run away."

Chandra swayed against Rick. "What?"

Rick's hands closed around her upper arms, supporting her. "What makes you think he's run away, Lillian? When's the last time you saw him?"

"I'd been busy in the studio"—she looked at Chandra—"you know, we talked. Well, a little while after Rick came to pick you up, I went up to Ty's room to check on him, and there was no sign of him. I thought at first he might be playing a game with me, but dinnertime passed, and it was dark, and the storm was coming in . . ." Completely distraught, Lillian wrung her hands together. "I tried to reach you at Rick's house, but no one answered."

Chandra gripped her mother's hands. "Calm down. We're going to find him. What really troubles me is that I can't imagine what would make him run away."

Lillian's eyes slewed accusingly to Rick. "I can. My guess is, he overheard you telling me that Rick was his father."

Chandra gasped. "Oh, no!"

Rick's face wore a grim expression. "Poor little guy."

The sound of a truck drew their attention toward the drive. "Is that Nolan's truck?" Rick asked.

Lillian nodded. "I called him. I didn't know what else to do. I sent him out to check the area where you all went that day to hunt arrowheads." She twisted her hands together. "Ty just doesn't know that many places around here to go."

Nolan climbed down out of his truck and immediately shook his head, indicating to them that he hadn't found Ty.

Fighting panic, Chandra turned back to her mother. "Where have you looked?"

"Everywhere! The house, the yard, the barn."

Rick interrupted her. "Did you give the barn a real thorough check?"

"I took a flashlight out there, walked through it, and called his name."

"Did you check the loft?"

Lillian shook her head. "I can't climb up there anymore."

"What's up there?"

Nolan was on the porch now, shaking the rain off his hat, and heard Rick's last question. "There's nothing up there but a bunch of boxes—storage, you know. I put them up there myself."

"Can I borrow your flashlight? I think it's worth checking out."

"I'm coming with you," Chandra said.

Rick took the flashlight from Nolan. "If we find him, I'll signal you by turning the flashlight on and off three times."

Once again they ran through the rain, only this time they weren't laughing.

Visions of Ty being lost, afraid, and possibly hurt, not to mention wet and cold, had Chandra praying harder than she ever had in her life. *Let us find him. Let him be in the barn. Don't let my son be hurt by my mistakes.*

Compared to the storm that raged outside, the inside of the barn was ominously quiet. Without wasting time talking, they hurried to the ladder that led up to the loft. Chandra went first, but Rick was close behind her.

When she reached the top, she swept the flashlight over the area. Her heart sank. There was no sign of Ty. Walking slowly forward, she sighted the boxes Nolan had told them about. A couple were open. Curiously, she looked closer. The boxes contained old blankets, and from the level of the blankets in the box, it appeared as if some of them might be missing.

From across the way she heard Rick softly call her name. She swung her flashlight beam toward him, and he motioned with his hand toward one corner of the loft. Switching her light to the corner, she saw Ty, huddled in a tight ball amid several of his most prized Transformers and a pile of blankets. The relief that flooded through her was so great, she almost stumbled over one of the boxes.

Rick went immediately to the loft window and signaled the house.

Reaching Ty, Chandra's first urge was to jerk him up into her arms for a fierce hug, but she restrained herself. Kneeling beside him, she saw that his small face was stained by tears. "Ty, honey, why didn't you answer Grandma when she called you? And what are you doing out here? You had us all scared to death."

He rubbed at his eyes with the heel of his hand, obviously not wanting her to see that he had been crying. Then he looked behind her and saw Rick. Immediately his expression changed, and he scooted into a sitting position. "What's he doing here?" he charged, anger and confusion throbbing in his voice.

"Rick helped me find you. He was worried too."

"I don't want him here," Ty exclaimed angrily, his inner misery showing clearly. "Tell him to go away!" Just then, thunder boomed overhead, and Ty jumped.

"You overheard me and your grandmother, didn't you, Ty?"

Rick knelt beside Chandra. "I can understand why you're upset, Ty, but running away was wrong."

Ty's bottom lip came out in defiance, but his chin quivered. "I thought you liked me!"

"I do."

"Then why, if you're my dad, didn't you ever come to see me?"

A child could be heartbreakingly logical, Rick thought, completely stricken by Ty's pain and bewilderment. "Because I didn't know that you were my son. I only found out tonight, just like you."

"Honey, how much of our conversation did you hear?"

"I heard Grandma say she wished she'd shot Rick!"

"That was the last thing you heard?" Chandra asked.

Ty nodded.

"Then you didn't hear me say that Rick didn't know you were his little boy, and you didn't hear me say I loved him."

"I don't *want* you to love him! We don't need him!"

Chandra had heard all the hurt in Ty's voice she could stand, and she gathered him into her arms. "Listen to me, honey. Listen! Do you remember my telling you that when I was very young, I had loved a boy and had become pregnant with you?"

Ty nodded.

"Well, Rick was that boy, and I left here without telling him that I was pregnant with you. He never knew until tonight."

"That's right," Rick said, "and I couldn't be happier about having you for a son." The expression on Ty's face plainly said he didn't believe a word that Rick was saying, but Rick kept talking in that soft, soothing way he had. "I had already grown to love you, Ty. I had even asked your mother to marry me. Do you understand? That means that I wanted to be your father *before* I found out that you were really my son."

Ty glanced up at Chandra for confirmation of what Rick was saying. Because her throat was clogged with emotion, she simply nodded.

Rick sat down on the other side of Ty, getting as physically close to him as he could without upsetting the boy any further. "I'd like very much for you and your mother to stay here in Monte Luna and live with me. We've got a lot of years to make up for."

Ty's gaze was wrenchingly solemn. "Are you really my dad?"

Rick swallowed hard. "I really am."

Chandra arranged blankets over them, and they talked for a long time. Eventually, with Rick and Chandra on either side of Ty, holding him and each other, they fell asleep. When they awoke, it was morning and the storm had passed. Chandra felt Ty stir beside her.

"Mom, can I go tell Grandma that we're not leaving and that I have a dad?"

She opened her eyes and smiled at him sleepily. "Sure, honey."

He wiggled out from between Rick and Chandra, then pushed himself up and gathered his Transformers together. Ty started off across the loft, but suddenly stopped. Turning around, he glanced shyly at Rick, who had been watching him. "Are you going to leave? I mean, are you going to be around?" He looked down at the tips of his boots. "I mean . . . am I going to see you again?"

Rick smiled reassuringly. "I'm not going anywhere, Ty, and you can count on that. Your mother and I will come down to the house in just a little bit."

"Great!"

After Ty had climbed down from the loft, Rick reached for Chandra and pulled her to him. "How are you?"

Unable to resist the urge, she rubbed her hand

over the night's growth of stubble on his cheek. "I'm wonderful, and this morning is wonderful, and I think you're wonderful."

He chuckled. "Well, that's certainly a comprehensive answer."

She made a halfhearted attempt to smooth out the wrinkles that had accumulated overnight in her aqua dress, then gave up, sighing contentedly because at last she knew what it was like to be truly happy. "I'm also indecently mussed."

"Now, that's an idea that I like very much—you, indecent." Slipping his hand under the top of her strapless dress, he dropped a warm kiss on her lips that lingered. "And I think you should know," he murmured, all the while caressing the soft flesh of her breasts, "that I'm going to buy Lillian the largest and nicest houseboat I can find."

Chandra could feel her breasts swelling in response to his touch. Needing to touch him also, she slid her hand inside his shirt until it rested over his heart. "A houseboat! Why?"

"So she can anchor it right over the spot where her present house is and paint to her heart's content."

Chandra laughed. "That's wonderful."

"You think everything is wonderful this morning," he murmured, unzipping her dress.

"Because it is"—she drew a shaky breath as her dress was pushed down to her waist—"and you have quite a creative idea, but you may not have to buy the houseboat."

"Why not?"

"Because any day, it's going to dawn on Lillian that Nolan's in love with her."

"Really?" He considered that while he twirled a nipple between his fingers. "She did call him when she needed help, didn't she? What do you think she's going to do when she realizes he loves her?"

"Run like hell." His mouth replaced his fingers. Chandra began to tremble. Yet she continued, her voice halting. "But Nolan strikes . . . ahhhh . . . me as a patient man. Without her even noticing . . . ooooh, Lord, that feels good . . . he's, uh . . . quietly ingratiated himself into her life. I'm betting he'll . . . Rick, right there . . . win her in the end . . . ohhh, yesss . . . !"

His hand left her breast to dip beneath her skirt. "Chandra?"

"What?" she rasped out, irritated. She didn't want to talk anymore. Need for him was rapidly taking over, blanking out all other matters.

"How do you feel about making love in the morning?"

"Wonderful," she whispered hoarsely, and pulled his mouth down to hers.

THE EDITOR'S CORNER

We have some wonderful news for you this month. Beginning with our October 1987 books, LOVESWEPT will be publishing *six* romances a month, not just four! We are very excited about this, and we hope all of you will be just as thrilled. Many of you have asked, requested, even pleaded with us over the years to publish more than four books a month, but we have always said that we wouldn't unless we were certain the quality of the books wouldn't suffer. We are confident now that, with all of the wonderful authors who write such fabulous books for us and all the new authors we are discovering, our future books will be just as much fun and just as heartwarming and beloved as those we've already published. And to let you know what you have to look forward to, I'll give you the titles and authors of the books we will be publishing in October 1987 (on sale in September).

#210 KISMET
by Helen Mittermeyer

#213 LEPRECHAUN
by Joan Elliott Pickart

#211 EVENINGS IN PARIS
by Kathleen Downes

#214 A KNIGHT TO REMEMBER
by Olivia and Ken Harper

#212 BANISH THE DRAGONS
by Margie McDonnell

#215 LOVING JENNY
by Billie Green

Before I go on to tell you about the delightful LOVESWEPTs in store for you next month, I want to remind you that Nora Roberts's romantic suspense novel, **HOT ICE,** is on sale right now. As I mentioned last month, it's dynamite, filled with intrigue, danger, exotic locations, and—of course!—features a fabulous hero and a fabulous heroine whom I know you will love. He's a professional thief; she's a reckless heiress looking for excitement. When he jumps into her Mercedes at a stoplight and a high-speed chase ensues, both Doug Lord and Whitney MacAllister get more than they bargained for! I'm sure you will love **HOT ICE,** so do get your copy now!

We start off our August LOVESWEPTs with Patt Bucheister,

(continued)

who has given us another tender and warm story in **TOUCH THE STARS,** LOVESWEPT #202. Diana Dragas can't stand reporters because they destroyed her father's career as a diplomat. This causes problems for the handsome and virile Michael Dare, who is captivated by the beautiful Diana—and is, alas, also a reporter. Still, Diana can't resist this gallant charmer and allows Michael to sweep her away. When she discovers he's misled her, she has to make the most important decision of her life. As always, Patt has created two wonderful people whom we can truly care about.

Peggy Webb's newest LOVESWEPT, **SUMMER JAZZ,** #203, is as hot and sultry as the title suggests. Mattie Houston comes home from Paris looking for sweet revenge on Hunter Chadwick, the impossibly handsome man who'd broken her heart years earlier. Both Mattie and Hunter are certain their love has died, but neither has forgotten that summer of sunshine and haunting jazz when they'd fallen shamelessly in love—and it takes only one touch for that love to be resurrected. But all the misunderstandings and pain of the past must be put to rest before they can be free to love again. This is a powerful, moving story that I'm sure you'll remember for a long time.

Joan Elliott Pickart has always been well loved for her humor, and **REFORMING FREDDY,** LOVESWEPT #204, has an opening that is as unique as it is funny. Tricia Todd never imagined that her physical fitness program—walking up the four flights of stairs to her office—could be so dangerous! Halfway up, she's confronted by a young thief, and she shocks herself as much as the teenager by whipping out her nephew's water pistol. She threatens to shoot Freddy, the young criminal, and gets more than her man—she gets two men. Lt. Spence Walker, rugged, handsome, and cynical, is certain that Tricia, a bright-eyed optimist, is all wrong for him. So why can't he keep away from her? And furthermore, what is she doing when she's mysteriously out of her office at odd hours during the day? Actually, Tricia is doing exactly what Spence told her not to do—reforming Freddy. You'll laugh out loud as Tricia tries to deal with both Freddy and

(continued)

Spence, teaching each—in very different ways—that they don't have to be afraid of love.

Next, Susan Richardson's **A SLOW SIMMER,** LOVE-SWEPT #205, pairs two unlikely people—gourmet cook Betsy Carmody and hunk-of-any-month quarterback Jesse Kincaid. Betsy and Jesse had known each other years earlier, when Betsy was married to another player on the San Francisco football team. That marriage was a disaster, and she wants to have nothing to do with the big, mischievous, and handsome Jesse . . . but he doesn't believe in taking no for an answer and just keeps coming back, weakening her resistance with his sexy smiles and heart-stopping kisses. This is a charming love story, and Jesse is a hero you'll cheer for, both on and off the field.

Do I need to remind you that the next three books of the Delaney Dynasty go on sale next month? If you haven't already asked your bookseller to reserve copies for you, be sure to do so now. The trilogy has the overall title **THE DELANEYS OF KILLAROO,** and the individual book titles are:

Adelaide, The Enchantress
by Kay Hooper

Matilda, The Adventuress
by Iris Johansen

Sydney, The Temptress
by Fayrene Preston

Enjoy!

Sincerely,

Carolyn Nichols

Carolyn Nichols
   Editor
LOVESWEPT
Bantam Books, Inc.
666 Fifth Avenue
New York, NY 10103